LITTLE RED TRANSISTOR
RADIO FROM TRIESTE

Little Red Transistor Radio from Trieste

Dragan Todorovic

ISBN: 978-0-9570984-9-7

For sale in the United Kingdom only

Scan QR code for further title information

A Hotwire Short Story Collection
First published October 2012 by:

Nine Arches Press
Great Central Studios
92 Lower Hillmorton Road
Rugby, Warwickshire
CV21 3TF

www.ninearchespress.com

Printed in Britain on recycled paper by:

imprintdigital.net
Seychelles Farm,
Upton Pyne,
Exeter
EX5 5HY
www.imprintdigital.net

LITTLE RED TRANSISTOR RADIO FROM TRIESTE

DRAGAN TODOROVIC

HOTWIRE

To my daughter, Ana

Dragan Todorovic is a writer and multimedia artist whose publications include eight books of non-fiction, poetry and fiction. He has worked extensively in print and electronic media, both in Serbia (where he was born) and in Canada (where he lived between 1995 and 2005). Some of his articles, books and artistic projects have won international awards.

Little Red Transistor Radio from Trieste is his first collection of short stories to be published in the United Kingdom.

CONTENTS

LITTLE RED TRANSISTOR
RADIO FROM TRIESTE

1969:

He lives in a slow town two hours south of Belgrade.
He is eleven years old and he's in love for the first
time. Several weeks ago a new girl had joined his
class. Her father is an actor who has recently moved
to town to work in the local theatre.

Their music teacher often turns her classes
into small concerts: anyone with a sudden urge to
perform can simply come forward, tell a few words
about the song he intends to sing, and start. One day
he gathers courage, stands up, and introduces
'Romana', a big hit of the leading Serbian singer.
While singing the opening verses—"Who stole the
night's darkest colours, wove them into your eyes and
gave them such shine"—he is standing in front of her
desk looking her straight in the eyes. They are azure,
not black.

The original singer of 'Romana' is famous for
taking off his jacket in the middle of the song and

throwing it passionately to the floor, but he feels it would be stupid if he took off his shirt and threw it away. He is ashamed of the white tank top his mother ordered him to put on that day. The real men do not wear them. If he looks like a child then his love, too, will seem childish.

After that, he considers himself an evergreen singer and sees his future in some of the many local festivals of easy listening music.

A few days later Radio Belgrade plays 'Yellow Submarine', a popular if silly song the DJ says, by some British rock group called The Beatles. He finds the melody interesting and starts whistling it.

Later that evening his dad, a factory worker, reads his newspapers in bed, as usual. On the photo news page there is an image of four guys in black suits and with funny haircuts, and Dad says to Mum, "Look at that scum! I'd give a haircut to all those beetles!"

He feels a strange distance between him and his parents.

1971:

Music comes to their home through a little red transistor radio his mum had smuggled from Trieste, Italy. After a couple of months of his persistent nagging, his father buys a Japanese mono turntable with AM radio.

Since both his parents work and he stays alone at home, they leave him money for breakfast. The amount is calculated so it buys a piece of pie and a glass of yogurt, but it also happens to be sufficient for a single. Occasionally, he buys records instead of food. The first one is Melanie's 'Lay Down'.

He considers transition from the red transistor radio to the well-designed Taya turntable a big step, both for him and the humankind. Since his best friend has had such a record player long before him, he decides to take one step further and buy his first album: The Rolling Stones, *Gimme Shelter*. He has to miss six breakfasts, but even then the money isn't sufficient. He discovers that the telephone booth on the corner often steals callers' coins, so he develops a special kick that sometimes forces the machine to spit out the money.

A friend from his class, considered an expert in English, says that the real meaning of the title of the Stones' LP is "give me some pussy."

"Look in the dictionary," he says, "'gimme' is 'give me', while 'shelter' is 'something beneath, behind, or within which one is covered or protected, as from storms or danger; refuge'. Obviously, it must be—pussy!"

They are thirteen years old and enchanted by such insolence. They conclude that "the level of freedom over there in England is incredible, since here, in Yugoslavia, such things are not possible at all."

He loves records mostly because they can be collected and because they last longer than the stickers the other kids collect for their albums.

His mother suddenly links his losing weight with the growing number of records in his collection, announces philosophically that "money shouldn't be spent on trash, when pie is important for growth," and forbids him to continue collecting singles.

He goes underground and starts hiding his secret vinyl on top of the wardrobe, not expecting that someone else might have the same idea. One day, browsing through his records, he finds something soft wrapped in a shiny aluminium foil. He opens it to see a thing reminiscent of a balloon, just slightly wet and with a funny little tail at the top. In front of the house full of guests he asks his parents what is it. Mom immediately starts emptying ashtrays, and Dad, after a long and pregnant silence, says in a strange voice, "It's a condom, son. I'll explain later, when the guests are gone."

1972:

His sexual education comes mainly through reading "Ask Your Doctor" columns in magazines. He is thirteen and a half and writes in his diary: "I am worried about the size of my sexual organ. If my sexual partner notices this during the necessary foreplay, I might become impudent."

The same magazines that publish his favourite educational column happen to have regular rock news and he incidentally becomes well informed. Of all the things he has read about rock, he likes most the caption he found below a picture: "The Allman Brothers Band with wives, friends, dogs, and select children."

Big international hit 'Mammy Blue' hardly touches him. He prefers David Bowie and his 'Starman', a song he has heard one night on Radio Zagreb.

Playing football, he experiences his first fight and feels like a man, although he didn't do well. One night he dreams about how a girl from his class opens her notebook during the break—they are alone in the classroom—he unzips his pants and puts his thing into her notebook, and she closes it...

In the morning he discovers that his underwear is wet and he knows what it is, but he feels stupid because his first intercourse, albeit in his dreams, was with homework.

A couple of days later, some friend—his voice full of admiration—talks about a guy who has all four albums of Led Zeppelin. They are not sold in the local stores, so he decides to start ordering records by mail from England. He finds the address of Cob Records, from Wales, puts cash into an envelope and orders The Temptations, *All Directions*. The record never comes.

1973:

He finishes primary school as the Student of the Generation and for this success his parents buy him a new turntable: Traviata, stereo model, made of white plastic. Just right for his collection of Led Zeppelin albums. He extends speaker wires, places the white boxes on the wardrobe and invents his little game: around midnight he steals out of bed and in darkness, at full power, plays only Robert Plant's long scream from Zeppelin's 'Whole Lotta Love'. When Plant's done, he takes the needle off the record, shuts the turntable down, jumps into bed and pulls the blanket over his head. By the time his parents get out of bed and all the lights in the building across turn on, he is asleep. Since the building is next to the city cemetery, rumours involving ghosts start spreading fast.

He learns to play 'Smoke on the Water' by Deep Purple on his guitar. He considers music festivals to be old-fashioned and decides not to perform live. Instead, he will only do studio sessions.

He starts to like slow songs, since the more slow songs you know the better you dance, and the better you dance the less you are lonely.

1977:

After finishing high school he goes to the Montenegrin part of Adriatic coast with his two friends. They stay there for a month and he meets the girl of his life. He enrols in the Faculty of Law but soon discovers that nobody cares whether or not he attends and adjusts his habits accordingly. He fails his first exam in January since his girlfriend is practising fellatio. A real music expert, he loves records because they remind him of tree rings: each groove is a memory.

1978:

He forms a band with two friends. On a tape deck made in Czechoslovakia they record three songs. Certain that one of them will be a big hit—

guaranteeing the success of their future first album—
they start planning their second record. They get
into an argument about the name of that other
project and the band falls apart.

That summer he spends two weeks in the
army camp, going through compulsory military
training for freshmen. He hates it with passion.
Once it's over he drives off to the coast with one
of the boys from his old band. It seems that on
every restaurant patio there is a third-rate band
performing disco hits and mouldy music. It is
practically standard nuptial music back where he
lives and he swears he will never play weddings.

During their stay the price of petrol goes up,
so they have to return earlier than planned. He is
with the girl of his life, but she is not the one from the
year before.

1980:

It's getting worse at the university. He claims that his
professors are idiots and that he doesn't want to let
them change his views. He rarely plays guitar,
horrified by disco. Meets a new girl of his life.
Discovers jazz.

One night he dreams of flying: while walking
down the street, he suddenly decides not to put his
foot to the ground again, and indeed, he starts to
fly. So, that is the trick: flying is only walking that is
not finished.

1982:

Not finishing a single step he takes, he still doesn't fly.

He is increasingly rebellious and then gets conscripted. He decides to chop off his right index finger, which would forever set him free from the army. There is an old cleaver in the pantry, and he finds it, but it is rusty. He gives up on self-mutilation and serves his term in a town close to the northern border, where the wine is old and the girls are wild. Contrary to all expectations, he feels good and silently joins the overwhelming majority of men who like to talk about their army days.

1983:

He is out of the army. Finds an editorial job with an underground magazine in Belgrade. He rarely buys records or goes to concerts.

The professor of history in his old high school commits suicide and that feels sad. He started loving history because of her. She gave him the feeling that history should be democratic; everyone should know it and anyone could create it.

Even more rebellious, he starts to study the events of 1968, the year of the international student unrest.

1984:

His interest in 1968 suddenly increases after he makes love to a girl born that year. Afterwards, smoking, he thinks how it was obviously a fiery year and then realises that he is ten years older than this baby. He pulls his stomach in, gets out of bed, and puts on Dylan's 'Señor'. After two minutes, she asks him if he could play something else instead of that lemonade. She would like something from Duran Duran, please.

That same night, after she has left, he gets dead drunk and goes to bed after three in the morning, blaming Orwell for everything.

1986:

Most of his friends are already married. Girls are treating him in two ways: either they think he is old, full of experience, and should be consumed for a night or two, or they think he is old, full of experience and a candidate for marriage. Running away from both, he turns more and more to music. He plays his old records deep into the night, smokes two packs a day, and plans a trip to Trieste, where he would buy just a little red transistor radio.

1988:

A growing number of people talks about resurrection of Serbia under the new leader. Reading Slobodan Milošević's biography in some magazine he realises that this man is Mick Jagger's generation, finds it funny and publishes a satirical piece ridiculing the politician. Several mornings later he gets a call from his boss's assistant informing him that he doesn't need bother coming to work again. Springsteen's 'No Surrender' is on the radio while he's talking to her. He hangs up, listens to the rest of the song and five minutes later calls a young publisher to propose a book he has never planned to write, a biography of Bruce Springsteen. That same afternoon they sign the contract and he spends next three months listening to Springsteen's records, drinking litres of coffee and writing fifteen hours a day.

1991:

He has two more books published but somehow things matter less now the war has started.

He takes part in huge protests that end with tanks on the streets in the evening. That night he suddenly understands that not only has his generation gotten its own war, they've gotten their own, lesser Hitler. He wants to be a hero, he's always believed in "better to burn down than to fade away," he wants to fight, but how? It's too late for satire, too early for snipers.

1992:

Finding his niche on a small radio station he creates a call-in show running Sundays between midnight and morning. He talks with his callers about sex, music, fear, hope, hunger, love... He keeps it simple and open and feels like a winner every Sunday morning, ending his show and looking down on the grey roofs of Belgrade: just to be able to talk about ordinary things in times when the media is full of war propaganda is a subversion. His two friends who work with him seem to be very proud of taking part in something so dangerous. They play officially prohibited Croatian and Bosnian music. He introduces a section of the show where he reads his own, much-politicised diary. All is perfect. He is waiting for the ban. Anything would do, he just wants an incident. He wants to cure the blind eye. If you work under the dictatorship and you've never been arrested, you've not pushed it far enough.

Around three one morning a girl with a very sexy voice calls in, obviously masturbating, and he lets her do it on the air. She's very poetic in her descriptions, but she really takes her time doing it. After twenty minutes of their steamy talk he sees two uniformed men entering the studio on the other side of the glass. Finally. But the two men just exchange some words with his friends and leave. His friend Nash leans towards the internal communicator on the console and says, "They just dropped by to say we're crazy, but they like it."

1993:

One day he opens his telephone book to find a guest for his show and realises that majority of his friends have emigrated in the last two years. In 1991 a couple he knew had left for Canada, then another for New Zealand, but it looked like isolated incidents. Apparently it has continued and he hasn't been paying attention. Many people who were his allies have left. Yes, the others and he are doing their little things in public life—slipping in a line in a daily, a story in a magazine, a provocative song on the radio—keeping the spirit of freedom alive, but what does it mean? Do dictators get even scratched by these little steps of mutiny? Are you a hero doing it, or just an ordinary guy staying true to yourself? Even if he would become a hero, somehow, who would be there to admire him when all his friends have left? Who would be impressed? Is there a hero without an audience?

Looking for the meaning of it all, he takes his remaining savings and travels to Barcelona. He stays in a run-down hostel near the coast, and the change of guards in front of some ministry across the street reminds him of Franco and Milošević, and confuses him even more.

Five days later it's his thirty-fifth birthday. He decides to buy a bottle of cheap champagne and drink it sitting on some steps in the harbour, just below the monument to Columbus. The next day he is going back to Belgrade and he still doesn't have a single answer to his many questions.

An old Spaniard approaches and sits quietly across from him, watching him roll the tobacco. He offers the Spaniard some wine, and the man accepts. The sun is testing water, the air smells of salt, September is beautiful on the sea, and the lines on Spaniard's face look like a map of wisdom. Here is the Deus ex Machina in flesh and blood, sitting silently as he talks at length about himself, about his dilemmas, small victories, betrayals, about scratching the doors of history. The Spaniard is smoking his tobacco, sipping his wine and occasionally nodding.

The sun is wet and the bottle is empty. The Spaniard offers to go and buy more wine, and he reaches into his pocket and hands him all the money he has left. He is half drunk and gods are expensive. And he is going back in the morning.

He waits for half an hour, then another half-hour, but the Deus never returns.

1995:

The war is over. Slovenia, Croatia, Bosnia—it's all gone quiet. Milošević is celebrated in the world media as the man of peace.

He quits his job with the radio station and becomes the editor of a porn magazine. His office is in a small shack in the publisher's backyard. His usual clients are hookers, ex-hookers, would-be-hookers, and their underfucked photographers. A thousand for an orgy, add two hundred for anal. He welcomes that simplicity. The immigration documents from the Canadian embassy arrive one day, but he just drops them into some drawer.

One day an ex-hooker comes to him and offers her diary for publishing. He is sceptical, but tells her to leave it with him for a couple of days. He takes the small blue notebook home and starts reading it in the evening, expecting to just flip through a few pages. It is Volume One, her high school years. She's a good student, pretty (true, some of it still shows), ambitious, and plans to conquer the world. Forms a band with two girlfriends (The Jolly Vaginas) and changes boyfriends like socks. At eighteen she falls seriously in love, and the guy cheats on her. Wanting revenge, she goes to bed with someone much older, and he—misjudging her—leaves a hundred in her jeans. That's how it starts.

He reads her diaries one by one in the coming days and starts publishing them. They become friends. Platonic. He's not asking, she's not offering.

After several instalments, she disappears. The police cannot find anything suspicious and suggest that she might have left for some foreign country, where johns are rich and hookers get happy. But he still has her two last notebooks, those in which she's described how she fucked politicians.

In November he packs some of his records, a copy of each of his three books, and some wardrobe. After a few bear hugs he is on the plane to Paris, where he will spend a night and in the morning continue to Canada. In a tightly-crammed electronics shop at the airport he buys a little red transistor radio. That night, in a cheap hotel room in Paris, he listens to Radio Belgrade. They introduce The Beatles, 'Yellow Submarine'.

CAMERA OBSCURA

He was a photographer who lived in a town that was sagging under too many refugees from life. His wife had some psychological malady. The episodes were not especially frequent—several months of hesitant silence in between the chapters—but they were unpleasant. She would get scared of large spaces, public squares, supermarkets, television, and her nerves would become like a skin scorched by the sun. It was impossible to hug or comfort her when she was like that—she was allergic to the world as a whole, not only to her husband's touch.

It would start with a single attack, then for a few days nothing would happen, until another crisis would hit, followed by a span of peace—attack, retreat, faster, faster... As with all such problems, after a while the malady stopped being an episode and started feeding on ever larger chunks of calendar, until days without symptoms became the slack; commas in a sentence which obviously hasn't been finished and where pain was added with every new word. One such cycle lasted for about two months.

The wife had originally been prescribed some medicine to return the pendulum of her happiness into balance, but she claimed that, with peace, came several other states she didn't like—indifference to everything, lack of ambition, dwindling of the libido. The bliss pills seemed to act like craving-statics, killing good desires with bad, zombifying her whole being. Every longing seemed to have been eliminated when doctors administered happiness.

She changed her doctor, and instead of continuing with the heavy medicine he advised her to go for a custom-tailored regime of natural supplements and yoga, teas and good books. It was a slow help, much slower than her original prescriptions—her new doctor had warned her—but it was safe and it left her personality in peace.

On quiet days the photographer took his camera and went for a walk on the outskirts of town. He was trying to find a concept for a book of photographs, which would—perhaps—contain short inscriptions, maybe as short as haiku. He hoped his wife could write those. She had published two collections of poetry before she met him and he always harboured a layer of guilt that she stopped writing after they got married and his career with the news agency really took off. Had he been around enough to support her—he thought—perhaps her problem would've been lesser, or she should've never had it. He specialised in covering natural disasters and his trips always involved a few weeks of absence at the time: the ruins, the bodies, the stench—the toccata of death; then the survivors, the help, the world—the sweet fugue of life. He hoped that solitude might help his wife write, but it didn't work that way. In fact, he didn't know much about what slowness did to creativity. Photography is about speed and stealing the moments away from it. After one long conversation with his wife, during which she mentioned this about speed, he decided to give a chance to nothing, to stillness, to the metaphysical, if possible. But that was just a general idea, not a theme, nothing sufficiently concrete. *That* he hoped to find on his walks.

Apparently, he wasn't one of those who walk to find the answers. The concept didn't come. At least he now had a healthy habit of spending hours in fresh air, in the memorial park on the outskirts and the wood that was part of it. It brought him peace, it was his meditation. Always carrying his camera with him, he continued to snap, almost automatically. These weren't photographs because he wasn't thinking about composition, these were only frozen moments.

He took pictures of whatever drew his attention. In a dense bush along the paths where he walked, what stood out was what was different in colour to the greenery. Sometimes it was a yellowing branch of a bush, a condom on a path, a woman's underwear joyously thrown over a branch of the highest tree (why always a woman's?), and sometimes it was a little patch of paper snow made of soaked tissues where a car had been parked the night before. Since he never left the switch of his camera on automatic setting, the images were often blurry, foggy, breathless, almost porous, as if it would be possible to cram into them yet more objects and details and thoughts—even when they had been wrapped up, developed, smelted into silver on paper.

Little by little, he started to shoot almost exclusively the remains of others people's passions. He didn't pause to think of what he was doing—he snapped, he developed, he stored away. Just when the old album was almost full of contact sheets and he was thinking of dedicating a Sunday to going through the little frames to see if there was something there, another one of his wife's spells put everything aside for a month.

But there was something positive about her latest episode: the patch was shorter than any other except the very early ones. It was possible that her alternative cure was working. Encouraged, his wife—knowing of his haiku idea, and liking it—started to write the seeds of future stories. To show her how important this was to him, he began shooting the compositions that fitted with what she had written. It was a reversal of the original idea, but the order of making elements of their project did not matter to either one of them. Occasionally, the couple discovered that a photo, which he had made as an illustration of one of her writings, was actually a great counterpoint to something else. They were glad when that happened, because it witnessed them being on the same wavelength, forging the rings of the same chain.

On the edge of town, where woods clandestinely enter the lonely yards to leave behind their shadows, there stood a house. It looked old-fashioned: dark terracotta tiles on the roof, a crumbling chimney in the back, and a large, shadowy veranda in front, with cracked wooden beams and window panes broken in places. It belonged to the local Museum, and it was built only some thirty years before, as a sample of the local traditional architecture. The project had been abandoned long ago and the house left to itself. Everything that could have been separated from the floor or the walls had been stolen. The front yard, once full of flowers and decorative bushes, now was covered with briars, wild roses, nettle and a selection of greens resilient to the slowly rusting beer cans. Although no one lived in the house, traces of life could be found inside. This being the farthest point of his walks, the photographer hid there a few times from the summer rain and he always found fresh butts and paper cups.

Over the months, he had become somewhat of an expert tracker. By the positioning and the quantity of the remains he found and photographed during his ramblings he could tell a few things about the couples that left them behind.

A pile of paper tissues, decomposed after only a night on the ground—a rainless night—told of an outpouring of a long-supressed passion, perhaps something secret. A best friend and his friend's girlfriend, or boyfriend. Muffled sounds of making love, no screaming, but someone in a swoon, or in the vicinity of a love-induced blackout.

At the opposite: a few almost dry white tissues

witnessed the couple who did it simply because it could've been done, because of a sudden chance for skin to meet other skin. They did not plan for it to happen, because they'd been busy sleeping with other people. A little joy here, a little joy there—small winds for dandelions' downy tufts.

Traces left by the road pointed at the lovers who didn't really want to hide, who didn't have any third persons in their relationship, and made love in the car because of the decency, or because they'd simply been bored of doing it in the shadows behind their buildings.

Condoms and papers thrown deep in the wood, at the end of the impossibly narrow passages where driving carried the danger of getting stuck but where tyre marks were still visible on the ground, betrayed serious events, and people who tried to hide their encounters even from themselves. Incestuous, or same sex lovers, a friend of the family and the daughter of his friends, a boss and his secretary, a student and his professor. The world over there, on the road, was the reality, and this here, hidden, in the shadows, deep in the wood, was their subconscious, their dream, the world behind their deaths but before their deaths. The photographer thought how his tracing sometimes had certain metaphysical qualities. Always? He wasn't sure about that.

Like all tracers, detectives, adventurers, researchers, uncoverers, the photographer started hoping, one day, to catch other people in the act of love. Police inspectors do not really wish to find the fingerprints, or the footprints in the snow, or the letter made of newspaper cut-outs—they would prefer to see the hand that strangles, pulls the trigger, or cuts the letters out, *that* hand *while* it does that. Again, the photographer did not want to become a voyeur in the usual sense. The traces of love were more interesting to him than the love itself. Was it the reason he wished to catch a couple in the act, to be able to read them better, those whose signals were not clear enough? Maybe that was a pure intellectual challenge? Poirot du Sperm? Maigret van der Coitus?

But no, no: it was something else. Any good photographer is a master of time, someone who can freeze a moment and then display it in the way that model ships are built inside bottles—accessible but impenetrable. He just wanted to prove to himself that all moments were potentially his, even those of the highest intimacy. He wanted to believe that any second could be caught by his art, had he wished so.

On a foggy morning in December he went for the usual walk. After a year of this, he knew what anthropologists should have known but didn't: selection of coital space is not as random as lovers would like it. The romantic thought is that a sudden outburst of passion makes things happen anywhere, even in a public place. But he knew better: the traces he kept seeing were located in very specific areas. At first he had thought that the same couples chose the same spots, but then—piece by piece—the evidence of the opposite started emerging: the stable couples liked to change their location, to try something new (perhaps this need for spatial variation was at the root of adultery?); it was the random, the occasional couples that frequented the same setting. It seemed that certain places, or perhaps the physical circumstances in general at some sites, caused the erotic reaction and removed the inhibitory mechanisms at once. Not all of these places were hidden, not all were safe for getting naked. Still. It was as if the magnetic fields of some spots caused the compass of human behaviour to start spinning madly. Location chooses libido.

This discovery made easier his life as a collector.

His walks, now, were not incidental, nor made on a whim. He had developed the need for his usual fodder, and to get this he went where he expected to get the most. He'd become a winter animal and he depended on sated lovers to leave him their crumbs.

The area surrounding the old, decrepit house was rather lucrative for his purposes. But the winter—which technically hadn't started yet—was approaching with a bite, and for two weeks already he hadn't found anything; some dubious traces, a few times, but nothing worth raising his camera.

He set off in the direction of the house. The first snow had fallen a few days ago, and in some places it had began melting when the current wave of cold set in. The morning was bitter. Although he was already in the area where the wood was dense enough to filter out most of the wind, the slivers of gusts occasionally drilled through his jacket. Everything around him was in a state of flux: the patchy fog, the patchy snow, the change of seasons, his wife's patchy health—everything. It wasn't a happy flow, but winter's embrace is often like that.

He tried avoiding unhappy thoughts like toreador avoids the judgments of others.

He spotted a silhouette ahead.

Red sports jacket and black trousers and a tuque—that's what he could discern from where he was. The person hurriedly entered the old house.

A lovers' meeting?

He hurried, not quite hiding, but trying to keep the blackened trunks between the house and himself. Such are the secret connections among people: as soon as someone tries to hide something, someone else will want to discover what it is.

He slowed down, trying to put his heavy winter boots onto the patches of snow, to avoid the dead branches on the narrow path. Suddenly, something sparkled on the side, at the very edge of his vision. He turned around, breathless, thinking that he had been caught sneaking, spying, so he was readily ashamed and preparing an explanation.

There was no movement, and he realised it was an object, somewhere among the trees. That surprised him. Being a photographer, he was always keenly aware of the light around him, and the morning had no rays that could bounce off anything. Even the snow barely glistened.

The shine came through a thick bush to his right and he craned his neck trying to see what it was. The only thing he could discern was that it was some metal object, almost fully covered by a small pile of snow that the wind had pushed off a branch above. He walked around the bush and approached the object. It was sitting on top of a rotting stump. He reached down and carefully brushed the snow off.

An old camera.

It looked like a strange, wonderful box made of brass and copper and bruised aluminium, with brass rivets holding it all together. He knew that model, he had seen one such at the photokina exposition in Köln, some years before. It was originally a camera obscura, without an objective. The light would enter through a tiny hole and the projection of reality would appear, hanging upside down and much shrunken, on the plate in the back. There was a mechanism for advancing the film, and a clever little system of levers to open and close the shutter. It was made in East Germany, in some small village, by a watch-repairer who was a photography enthusiast, and the story went that there were about 30 of them in the world. The man had died in the meantime, making his cameras extremely expensive. It wasn't only because they were no longer made: the creator had made a remarkably good camera, which also happened to be a hauntingly beautiful object. The photographer was holding a small fortune in his shaking hands.

Somebody who owned this piece of art had modified the box, removing the drilled piece of metal in front and replacing it with an objective. But the objective was unknown to the photographer and was made of aluminium like everything else, so it was possible that this camera was an unknown work of the original inventor. In which case it must've been invaluable.

He looked around, expecting to see someone's footprints in the snow, or a frozen body somewhere near, but there was nothing. Silent black trees and snow and wind.

He slowly pressed the shutter and felt the mechanism moving as if it hadn't been standing in the snow for... how long? Remarkably, the click was inaudible. He tried turning the brass wheel on top of the camera and the light resistance told him there was a film inside. In cold weather like this, he was sure the film had kept well and hoped that, with a little luck, he could find something, some clues regarding the camera owner once he developed the pictures.

He hid his precious find in his jacket and proceeded towards the house. Without trying he walked very quietly now. His feet kept finding spots on the patchy ground where his boots produced only a whisper.

He was there, crouching under the broken window, before he knew it. He could hear faint and rhythmical sounds from the inside, but he didn't dare stand up to bring his eye to the corner of the window. He felt exposed, and just knew he had to do something fast.

Maybe a minute passed like that, or three, or five. The wind increased and the hum around him suppressed faint noise coming from the inside. But something was going on, and he couldn't just hide there. Slowly, he straightened and leaned his face against the frame.

A man and a woman in a tight, desperate embrace. They moved around the room, holding each other firmly, his stubbly cheek against her fresh, tense face. Her eyes were closed—pain or elation? They moved not quite in unison, as if still learning how to comprehend each other, or as if carefully keeping their differences.

To the photographer it looked like tango, or some similar choreography of delusion and pain. Except that there was no audible music, there was only the flow they shared in their heads.

He lifted his camera to the corner of the window, but then realised it would make too much noise for this situation. He pushed it back on his shoulder, took out his newfound camera and pointed it blindly. He pressed the button. Again. Several times. Not wanting to risk being noticed, he crouched once more and carefully went behind the house and then between the trees, until he reached his path.

At home, his wife waited to show him the new stuff she had written the previous night. He was faster: he showed her the brass camera, kissed her on the cheek and hurried into his darkroom to develop the film. She was disappointed, but not too much. In fact, she liked him when he was excited like this, liked his energy. It's one of the things she has been missing from their marriage for the past few years.

She made a coffee and sat down to read her entries again. She had the impression she was finally getting somewhere interesting and now she felt a big push, a surge of enthusiasm for this book he had proposed. She liked the voyeurism of his images — and for the first time she felt sure she succeeded in making her words have the same quality. A rabbit caught in the headlights is surprised and a surprise. A couple in action is both the subject and the object.

She felt that this was the key: the same way his images were not properly sharp, focused — her words did not have to catch the vista in its entirety. Voyeurs are not interested in witnessing the details; they are focusing on the energy of the moment, of the act. They are watching their proxies performing something that belonged to them, their own show they were prevented from attending. Voyeurism is an out-of-body experience.

And she had finally found her out-of-body words.

In the darkroom, he was poking the papers in the plastic tub with his tongs. The red light soothed him. This was the moment he loved: when the transparent liquid revealed the picture that had been hidden in the white. There was something both old and new in that. He felt like an engraver, as if he held a needle and a copper plate was laid before him.

He was keen. He had already seen that the film in the camera was a top-quality black and white brand, of high sensitivity. Such film tends to produce grainy images, with higher contrast and dramatic shadows. But a good camera does affect this, and he was curious to see if the photographs that came out of this old box matched its external beauty.

As the dark areas formed on paper, the couple reappeared like a memory found in an old ticket. He didn't expect much from this last one: they had been very close to his camera, and so the element of bodies in movement was lost. He could hardly wait now for this one to be done, and he moved it from the developer to the stop bath and then to the fixer with a sigh of relief.

The rest of the papers were already under the

flow of water, and he picked the last image and placed it on top of the others. And then it drew his attention. He brought it closer to his eyes: it was obvious—the woman had spotted his camera. She was looking straight at the lens. In the corner of her eye was a tear, and there was a shiny path down her cheek. The man's face was turned in the same direction, cheek to cheek, but his eyes were looking down. Along the line where their cheeks touched, a shiny path flowing from her other eye glued them together. His lips were pressed tightly, his mouth an old cut that wasn't bleeding anymore.

The photographer stood in his darkroom, staring at the wet paper in his hand.

Accessible, but impenetrable. Love.

He'd finally found his lovers from the wood. To him, it was not the particular couple, not any special couple; they didn't have names—they were representing everyone who has ever despaired and disappeared in that forest. To him, it was like decoding the genome of love.

He switched off the small red transistor radio he usually had on when working and turned the tap off.

He came out of the dark room with trepidation. He was a beggar with a small plastic tub in his hands, the washed pictures swimming inside.

He put the tub on the coffee table and took out a paper, holding it at the corner with his tongs. His wife took it from his hand and looked at it, while his eyes rested on hers, keen to catch her immediate reaction, her early face.

But her first face surprised him: she looked lost in thoughts, and then puzzled. Now he was confused and he sat next to her on the sofa. Maybe he had made a mistake when developing the prints. Maybe the chemical was too old—he hadn't checked the date on the bottle. Maybe one of the substances spoiled another, drops coming off his hand. It had happened a few times.

He brought his head close to hers, almost cheek to cheek, and looked over at the paper.

"What?" he asked.

"There is something strange in this," she said slowly, as if trying to liquefy the fog of her early impressions.

"What's strange?"

"There is such a frown on his face... Look at it: like a razor, that sharp. Why? He's practising his dancing steps, but this doesn't look like him concentrating."

"Perhaps it's because of her."

"I agree," she said, "there must be a *her*. But his emotion is so raw, and he's dancing alone. In the ruins in a wood. And look—he's crying. How insane is he? How wounded?"

Alone? He didn't even know what she was talking about.

He kept staring at the picture, then at her, then back at the paper. The woman in the frame was looking at him, a tear in her eye.

He took the photo from her hand, to inspect it closer.

The brass camera made astonishing images considering how old-fashioned and in some ways primitive it was. The contrast was softer than the film sensitivity would dictate, the details were strong, and on top of it all there was something warm, something special and deep, something that gave each frame a narrative. It was as if the camera had a personality.

He raised the image for her to look again. He started commenting on various details, pretending to talk about the quality of the photo, wanting to see if something else had remained invisible to his wife. She could see everything but the woman. The area that the woman's body covered in the picture was as invisible to her as it was to him—only, he saw a body hiding it and she saw some shadowy area where there were no details and thought it was his artistry.

Obviously, it was her condition again, only this time it manifested itself differently. Psychological problems shift and snake like underground waters, always eroding and searching for a new and unpredictable way to resurface. Being erratic, they protect themselves from all cures, just like viruses, and earthquakes, and revolutionaries.

He didn't say anything about this to her. Instead, he carried the tub back to his darkroom, then asked to see her writings, and she gladly obliged. She took a handful of photographs from her desk and gave them to him. Small white pages from her notebook were attached to his pictures. He started flipping through them, and then went back and started reading.

Seemingly, none of what she had written had any link to the images it was coupled with. At first he thought she'd made a mistake and got them all mixed up, but then he saw what she had done: none of the sentences were clear, none used any word that would describe the objects in the frame. His objects walked on one side of the street, her words on the other. But it was clearly the same street. He couldn't remember seeing any book of photographs, ever, containing something as intelligent as that. Such beauty.

Such beauty. Such pity.

The next day the photographer went to see his wife's doctor. The doctor was their generation, and knew them through some mutual friends—that was why they had chosen him. He wasn't relying upon only one line of thought. He belonged to the new breed of doctors, who wanted to learn acupuncture and hypnosis and wanted to use belladonna with penicillin. Compared to her old doctor, a senior expert from the local hospital who just wanted to scan her brain and fill her up with happiness-inducing drugs, this man was as much a shaman as a doctor.

As usual, the doctor received him in the small office at the end of the corridor on the 9th floor of the hospital. A nurse had made a coffee and they chatted a little. Then the photographer told him about the strange episode from the previous day and, to illustrate, he took out the picture of the lovers from the wood. The doctor looked at it and said, "Wrong one. This is some man's solo," and pushed it back across the table. "He could use some sedative," he said. "Or a laxative," he added, and laughed.

The rest of the meeting went in a blur. The photographer was calm enough to tell the other man that he, indeed, had made a mistake and didn't bring the picture with him. The doctor told him to watch his wife for these same symptoms and to bring her to see him if they reappeared.

At home, alone since his wife had gone to her yoga class, he opened the wooden box where he'd put the mysterious camera, took it out and laid it on his light table. He switched on the lamps and adjusted the arm holding the magnifier to take a good look at the object.

On the outside, nothing was strange except for the choice of materials. Magnified, the camera looked even more magnificent. Every screw, every hinge, every curve had been done lovingly and with great precision. It looked as good as new. There were no visible scratches and, except for one spot near the shutter button where there was a slight change in colour on the copper—probably where the previous owner used to hold his finger—one could think this was a new camera, made for him, left for him to find it.

To do what for him?

He opened the door at the back of the camera and continued to look for something, anything. The usual stuff: the film capsule compartment, the lead on the other side, the protective membrane... No dust, no traces of use, nothing.

To do what to him?

He unscrewed the lens and discovered a system of mirrors underneath, inside the body of the camera, like no other he had ever seen. Normally, there would be a small looking-glass there, serving to reflect the image to the viewfinder before the shutter was pressed, when it would move aside temporarily. But in this case, there was a system of polished steel plates, interconnected in such way that they created all sorts of reflections, some distorted, some turned upside down, some even partial.

Perhaps that was ingenious, but it was still serving the same purpose: shrink the reality outside and lay it on the film. Catch it so it doesn't escape.

To do what around him?

At the back of the door there was just a small platform, pushed forward by springs, to hold the film container in place. There was an inscription on it, in very small letters, probably a warning. Nothing unusual, anywhere.

Just as he almost closed the door, he changed his mind and moved the metal so the miniature inscription was in focus. *Si tangit mysterium vobis nolite timere.* He got up to find his wife's small Latin dictionary on the shelf. He spent the next ten minutes trying to translate what it meant, and the best he could do was, 'Do not be afraid if the mystical touches you.'

Late in the night—when his wife was already in bed—he tried to find something about that strange inscription, but there was nothing, neither in the books nor online. He wanted to learn more about the man who had made the camera, but the details were sparse: born then, lived there, died then.

Before going to bed, he again took the writings that his wife had left on her desk. He read them slowly, and enjoyed them. He was moved, but it was a good excitement, a tingling, promising feeling, great to take with him to bed. He stood up and started to walk, pacing the room, rolling her words in his mouth like bonbons: it felt good.

From a certain spot in the room the large mirror by the entrance could be seen. He stopped suddenly, frozen. He couldn't see himself in the mirror. He put down the papers, his hair electric, his skin cold. Nonsense—he could see himself, of course. What an idiotic idea.

Then a thought zoomed into his head, and he took his wife's writings and stood in front of the mirror again.

There was nobody in the glass.

She was a writer whose husband had occasional panic attacks. Thankfully, the episodes were not frequent, but they were dramatic. He would get scared of small spaces, of mirrors, of television, even of his darkroom, and he had to concentrate hard not to show too much of his fear. That concentration sharpened his features and his face continued to hold that serious expression inbetween the episodes. It became a sharp face, rustproof.

During the attacks, he would become so tense, so frightened, that his skin would take on the pale colour of undeveloped film. The afternoon light, broken through the blinds, drew shadows of lost memories on his face. She tried holding him, she tried pressing her cheek to his cheek, but he didn't like it.

She worked in the local Museum. The salary wasn't much but then their demands were modest. Besides, he had found an expensive camera, and then—after he fell ill—he sold it to an American collector for a crazy amount of money.

She thought that the whole thing with the camera was very lucky; for some reason he thought it was a bad episode. In any case, they had enough for him to not have to go away every time a catastrophe struck somewhere in the world.

The only thing that calmed him down was browsing through his old pictures. His favourites were those first images taken with the brass camera. When looking at them, he felt he was inside that abandoned house.

WHAT I'VE SEEN

On Warwick Road, close to the train station, stands a man on the poorly lit sidewalk. His dun coat is held together by pieces of high-visibility tape. A knitted hat of indistinguishable colour and age and shape is crooked to the right. The man holds bags in both hands and stands there frozen in the middle of movement. It is possible that he might have forgotten where he was going. Or that he remembered something terribly important. Or he was suddenly struck by the illogicality of it all and realised that moving was as senseless as standing frozen in time, but that he could stand frozen longer and with less energy. Maybe he was waiting for his moment of dying, and I was the only one who saw him. Maybe he doesn't exist, he's never existed, and the reason I saw him is that I am an illusion as well.

His name is Marek. His name is Jim. His name is Dragan and I am one with him.

His given name is Nyx, his family name Night, and those of us who can see him have a different sight.

Cold December rain leaves no time to think. He has been caught in the beams of my car and was expecting me to kill him, but I wasn't up to my task. Now his universe, parallel to ours, will suffer. Stars will implode into black holes that will keep on devouring each other until they reach a total of eighteen, nebulae will become more nebular and turn into fairways, sand-filled bunkers and ponds full of cosmic balls. And all of that thanks to my near-miss.

I am afraid to drive on Warwick Road again.

From now until my last day the man will stand, frozen, on the same spot. His head turned to the right and bowed a little. Around him will always be this night. December, rain, deaf silence.

This night is not like others—a simple absence of day. This is a blot that is leaking from a very old quill, spreading over fields and fears, over love and loss, over teeth and tears. Ordinary nights spread in a uniform and predictable way, sneaking in behind our back while we're watching the sunset, progressing from there, too fast to fight them, too mild to realise the danger, and they cover everything that exists— living, unliving, soft and hard, growing or shrinking. This night, however, comes from several directions at once and goes wherever it wants. It can sidestep a town—if it feels like that—or a whole country, and it can double the darkness over another place. It doesn't cover everything and it certainly never covers everyone. It is a measure of a sort: if you are taller than the night, you will remain in light.

"Can you hear me, love? Here, I've brought this pretty card with blue Christmas lights on a silver tinsel tree decorated with sugar fairies and chocolate Santas. It is the closest I could find to our old tree. Remember that?"

On this same night in December, on the hill named Svetinja, which in Serbian means Holy, the rare drivers hurrying home notice that there is an unexpected cloud of thick fog covering the southern side of the elevation. Everywhere around the hill the sky is clear and the stars twinkle, diamondiferous and frigid, everywhere the wind is shearing, but as the road reaches the top and starts descending towards Kragujevac, a sharp curve leads straight into the cloud.

It is not large, perhaps a few hundred metres in diameter, and some of the drivers don't even have time to turn their fog lights on. What is easily passed is easily forgotten, and so nobody notices—except me—that it is not fog at all. It is a nebula from another dimension. All those who drive south, from Belgrade to Kragujevac, have to forget an event in their lives when passing through it. All those going in the opposite direction have to acquire a false memory. The number of records in private histories is limited. In fact, it is a constant in the known universe, one of the very few universal numbers, but nobody knows about it because nobody cares.

Obviously, both groups lose part of their lives. For those who have to forget one piece of their puzzle, one period of their lives, it is as if they have lived a shorter life. Those who "remember" will have to abandon some other, true experience; less will have happened to them.

The reason why I'm the only one noticing this mixing of universes is that I am not there. I am not passing through that sudden cloud, or nebula, or whatever that might be (and it could be an infinite number of things). Because I am far away, in a warm room lit by blue Christmas lights on a silver tinsel tree decorated with sugar fairies and chocolate Santas, I can clearly see that hill and what is happening there.

On the side of the road, a woman stands wrapped in fog. She is not invisible, but the drivers— surprised by the sudden whiteness—are too busy keeping their eyes on the road. One or two have seen her by pure chance, because they took their eyes off the road to find their cigarettes. She is a blonde. She's a brunette. She wears a headscarf. She is remarkably beautiful. She is old and wrinkled. She is a hooker. A mother. No, she is a ghost. Meat.

She doesn't raise her hand or make any other gesture that would suggest she needs a lift. She isn't even looking at the passing vehicles. Her head is slightly bent to the left, as if she's trying hard to hear something. She remains in that position, frozen, extemporal. Then a small white car passes hesitantly by and the light of its headlamps reflects against something small and shiny in her hair, some sort of a decoration.

Perhaps she is trying to remember something.

Nobody knows for sure why that hill was named Holy: there was never a church on it, so the name must be older than all the religions we know.

"Can you hear me, dad?"

A thousand kilometres away from there, in Regensburg:

Across from the cathedral, on the central square of that small German town, there is a hotel. It serves only breakfast in the small room that probably used to be an office, and in the evening there shouldn't be anyone in that space. Yet, there are two people sitting at the table close to the large gothic window. They are not facing each other, they are sitting shoulder to shoulder, both turned towards the facade of the cathedral. The architectural lights on the imposing old building reflect on their faces, and it's not clear whether they wanted to sit in the darkness and the light is bothering them, or if they intended to bask in the reflected light and it's the darkness that they dislike. Neither can it be known what they are talking about. I know it, but it must not be known.

Are they allies planning to take over the world? Are they enemies, brought here by people whose interests have been endangered by their fighting, to try and negotiate peace? Are they tired waiters waiting for tyres to be fixed on their car? Are they only a metaphor, and if so—what kind of metaphor? Fresh or stale?

In the low, narrow corridor leading to the kitchen there is a shelf and on it a cheap portable disc player and a little red transistor radio next to it. From one of these comes Shostakovich's *Second Waltz*. The volume is turned down, the music is barely audible, but it is so beautiful that even a mild exposure to such radiation can leave consequences.

I am afraid for those two: they've been listening to such music for a few hours already, and the nights in this southern part of Germany are long and murderous.

I've counted seven degrees of pain. Others will have known more, or fewer than that, so my experience is probably not transferable.

Then there is the speed of throbbing: some people react faster than others, and some have a lower threshold. For some, pain comes like a firestorm, senselessly fast and omnivorous, and for others it is like the stab of a long sword.

There are many colours of pain. For me, the strongest aches are red-brown. The body has no answer to that. Once I experienced malachite cramps, and they are awful as well, but I fear the red-brown combination.

At the 1st degree of pain—something everyone feels relatively often—the majority don't even take painkillers. That is our ordinary visitor, our friend and protector. Listen to your body now: isn't there a slight pain somewhere? It comes to tell us that the balance has been broken, that there is something we need to correct in our body. We deal with it by taking a walk, or pulling the shades down, or by moving, trying to find a more comfortable position.

At the 2nd degree we do take painkillers, and we reach for more serious measures. We quit working, we take a rest in a darkened room, we tie a scarf around our forehead. This degree is already not a warning but an early step into a disease.

At the 3rd degree, we reach for the strongest painkillers available to us, and we have no time to read the manufacturer's warnings about counter indications. We are more likely to seek help on this level of pain, and we send out clear signals that the pain is winning and the body is losing. That signal— be it verbal or just a sound, like moaning—is universally accepted as an SOS situation. Others, when they receive our signals, will likely try to help.

The 4th degree of pain is our last conscious plateau. We send out, if we still can, the most serious warnings to our surroundings. The scruples are gone, our principles defeated by the survival instinct. Screams and panic are common, losing control as well. We need help and we need it now. The level of pain is so high that the whole brain is affected by it, and even the signals that control the heart rate are jumbled, causing it to palpitate and increase the panic.

At the 5th degree we faint.

The 6th degree is a coma.

The 7th degree is impossible to describe. No one who has experienced it has come back to tell about it.

I am a doctor as well, not only someone who is a target, and I could talk about pain for hours. I could claim that there are smells associated with different kinds of aches (and there are—these are hallucinations, of course, but to the aching person they are as real as anything), that each sort of stabbing has a different colour and that it is, yet, different from throbbing... I could talk at length about it, as you surely understand.

But the simple truth is: a little pain is good, much pain is bad. Pain kills your thoughts, your relationships, the very essence of you. It devours everything, it is aggressive and merciless.

Pain is black, damp and mouldy. It stinks; it is full of worms.

"Pay attention to his lips."

"The blood? Probably from biting them."

"Are you starting him on this new stuff?"

"We already have. We don't have many other options left. I'm expecting the levels to achieve the plateau tonight."

At first it is all hazy and confusing, almost impossible. When the pain comes your body shuts all the exits very fast. It needs to focus on the fight ahead. It is trying to conserve what energy it has, because it needs it all to fight the pain. Your intellect runs in circles, trapped, surrounded by its own body, under a terrible attack. The mind is not really useful when you ache—it is only a relay, a knot of neurons and not a thinking machine. When one area of the body is in danger of something, it sends pain signals to the brain, and the brain passes the information on to all organs to start a war against the intruder, whatever it is—a virus, bacteria or a tumour. There is no thinking when in pain. There is only one thought: how to stop it.

If they're torturing you, tell them anything. If there is some medicine, take it. If it's the strange growth on your finger that is drilling through your brain, chop the finger off.

But I've discovered that if you force your mind to ignore the pain after the very first attack, and if you can do it fast, there is a good chance that your mind will abandon the body in time. The body slams all the gates shut, and one of the gates is somewhere in your neck. The mind that has gone out to roam will not be able to return for as long as the body is under attack.

You can stay anywhere, you can drive, fly, run, dive, you can be everywhere. You're invisible, you are anything you want to be. If you're fast enough, if you're brave enough, if you know when to leave your body. If you're heartless enough to leave your pretty profile, your long perfect fingers, your tower of pleasure, your well of desire, your lush skin—and all you can do with those.

"He has slept almost through the entire night. It hasn't happened in a while. God knows he needs rest. That new medicine seems very good."

"He hasn't much strength left in him."

"I know that. I just wish he could find enough strength to go in peace, with dignity... To tell us a few words, hold my hand, such stuff."

"I understand."

"Hopes shrink here, doctor."

Regensburg. December night.

The snowflakes drift very, very slowly. They appear like ordinary crystals until you look closer and you realise that they are the size of coffee cup saucers—the Turkish kind. They are not falling from the sky, but from the top of the cathedral. (Only this square and its immediate surroundings are affected. Down by the Danube, around the stone bridge and elsewhere, the night is quiet and dry.) It must be some remarkable new material that allows them to be so light and so unimaginably beautiful in their fall. Some of them can actually go up—a little—when close to the street lamps. Perhaps they react to the heat. Then they fall down, like all the others.

Now that the light from the street is multiplied the shadows are growing as well.

The couple in the small breakfast room are still sitting close to each other. I can now reveal this much: he is talking and she is listening. What she is hearing is not the same story that he is telling her. Now that you know that, you know that she is in love with him.

Does he love her?

Much more often than one would expect on a night like this in a sleepy town in the south of Germany, a car passes by, making a terrible noise while driving over cobblestones. These passing lights sometimes ricochet. One, just now, has hit the brim on a street lamp, rebounded in the direction of a spoonful of sugar in the right hand of a studentess sitting in the window of a torte shop next to the hotel, scratched a nickeled window frame of the parked car, and recoiled into the hair of the woman sitting in the small room. There, it finds something that reflects light and her hair shines for a second.

The same car goes further down the street, turns right on the corner and then, a few metres later, turns left. While passing by the window of the Antiquitäten Müller, its headlights disperse more light and a lost beam falls on a small clay figure of an angel in the window. The figure has been standing there for several months. The set price is not small, and angels are not en vogue. However, what are several months compared with 4,000 years? Nobody knows that the small figure depicting a man with bull's neck, hands of a blacksmith and rigid, sharp wings does not represent an angel, but Azazel, in his time known as The Teacher. In the green valleys below Mount Hermon, Azazel taught men the art of warfare, of making swords and shields, and he taught women how to decorate their bodies, and apply make-up, and dye their hair. The Book of Enoch says that in the end he was, at the Lord's command, chained to the jagged rocks, where he remains in darkness waiting to be thrown into the fire on the Day of Judgment. But one must not put too much faith in books. They consist of letters and it is not in vain that letters are like snakes.

Under the beam of reflected light, Azazel blinks.

Occasionally, I can hear the people around me. Most of the time they say trivial things and I am not expected to participate. Sometimes they come up with something sad, and I know that—

theoretically—I should react to that, to alleviate the pain, theirs and mine, but I can't find the place inside me from which my answer should come.

So I prefer to roam.

I cannot go back and forth in time. I can see and know only what belongs to my days—but my "eyes" are now all-accompanying. I can see everything at the same time, because it was my body that jailed me, and my eyes that blinded me.

I am new on these roads, but so is everyone else. The others I have met so far are as confused and as delighted as I am. Needless to say, we communicate easily now that we are liberated from language.

One of them has warned me of that danger, that trap where the majority of us Passagers seem to get caught:

Everyone has some period in their lives when it was great, or less painful than usual. We tend to stick to that era. Our memories get erased if they don't belong to that specific drawer, our sense of time dissolves. We live forever in that one pocket. We live happily ever after with the mirror framed in filigree made of our veins, the mirror that shows only one picture: us, when we were strong, us, the prettiest of them all.

It is not unnatural to go often to that happy place, he has told me, but you must travel elsewhere, too. It is one thing to keep returning, and something quite different to only make short absences so it looks like you've been elsewhere.

"Dad, can you hear me? Can you hear me dad?"

That car, slowly driving through Regensburg, with its headlamps shedding light, beams ricocheting in all directions—it is a Zastava 750. It is a small white car. It was manufactured in 1972, in the factory where my dad worked as an engineer, and he had personally asked some colleagues of his to follow one particular automobile from start to finish as it was his present to me for my 18th birthday. People in Yugoslavia were not rich at all at the time, and it was a sacrifice on his behalf that the whole town talked about.

The license plate is KG★136-64.

One night, maybe a year and a half after I got the car, I drove to some theatre show and parked the car in front of the theatre, in a well-lit place. When I got out, after the show, the car wasn't there. My friends and I searched the whole area. At first we thought that I forgot to pull the handbrake and someone had simply pushed the car to a hidden, dark place somewhere close, to have a joke on me. We couldn't believe it was stolen, because who would steal a small slow car like that, and where would they run away with it? But it was stolen. Two nights later, a police patrol knocked on our door to tell us they'd found it on the side of the road, on the outskirts of town. Was it badly damaged? No, it wasn't, I could probably drive it back after I pulled it out of the ditch. When a friend of mine drove me there, we discovered that the car was destroyed. It seemed too expensive to fix it, so we sold it to a mechanic who lived nearby, for parts. The car was taken apart and thus ended its life much the same way as a person does.

Later, when I thought about it, I decided that the small white Zastava 750 was like a rock star, one of those from the early seventies: lived fast, died young, had a pretty corpse.

Tonight I put it back together again, and I'm behind the wheel. I am the one who is salting all these events.

It is the same car I drove on Warwick Road. It is the last automobile on the Svetinja hill.

Azazel stretches his arms, then his torso. He hates it when others spread their wings—it's a show-off and vanity and nonsense. Some are born with wings, some without. What's there to brag about?

He belonged to an ancient tribe that once lived high in the mountains. When they were many they flew with eagles and they called themselves simply Flyers. Then came the Prophets who called Azazel's tribe Angels. They also said that his people lived in the skies, next to the gods in the beginning, and next to God later, and that they decided on everyone's destiny.

That changed everything. Azazel didn't like that and he, together with a group of his loyal friends, protested against such lies. But majority of the Flyers let their vanities rule them—they quite liked their new status of courtiers to the deities. It gave them importance, and power. Disgusted, Azazel led his group away. They had flown for days before settling in the Alps and the deep dark northern woods.

Many years later, several of the old tribe found them and told them about the big tragedy that befell

Flyers after Azazel and his friends left:

In the beginning, people respected and bowed to Angels. They offered them all sorts of gifts to mollify them and to ask them to plead in their name with the gods. But one day there had been an accident and an Angel was killed. Seeing that Angels bleed was the beginning of the end.

Since nobody was happy with their lives, people started attacking Angels, started accusing them of causing all their misfortunes. Instead of pleading with them, they started demanding from them. When their lives, of course, did not improve much, they chased them away and shot them with arrows, killing them. It became impossible to trade with people. Flyers had to withdraw and live an isolated life, but it is impossible to live like that. They dispersed all over the world and hid.

Azazel hears the conversation in the small breakfast room of the hotel a hundred metres away. And he knows what to do.

He leaves the store through the back door. Two Sumerian statues standing guard by the door salute him. Azazel frowns.

"You are not Ung Sang Gig-ga," he scoffs.

Going up the deserted street he is not trying to hide. His wings are tightly pressed against his body, giving him warmth and secrecy. With his muscular body and his strong neck, he looks like a bouncer and two young men who appear from the side street— tipsy a little judging by their voices—hurriedly cross to the other side.

He enters the hotel through a side window, then tiptoes down the corridor, gets to the first floor by stairs and finds the breakfast room.

The man and the woman inside are now silent. The music is different. I recognise Mahler's Fifth, that painful moment where everyone starts to cry. Azazel stands by the entrance, in the thick shadow of a pillar, listening. He is not looking for words but for silences between them.

After a while another car passes by and he uses the noise to move further into the room, behind them, then past them and into the narrow corridor leading to the kitchen, where the disc player spills the music onto the floor.

"It's good news—his results this morning are better. But please take this with a grain of salt. Our line of health is much like an ECG, it goes up and down all the time."

It is difficult to hear anything distinguishable in Azazel's voice. The music has changed in the meantime and it's Satie now. It is the first of his *Trois Gymnopédies* and every note trickling from the speakers hesitates on the edge of immense sadness.

Azazel is sitting with the couple. His back is turned to the window and only his silhouette is visible—the light from the cathedral is too strong to read his face. He is silent, except for a word or two he utters from time to time. Without trying to understand—one of the things you learn in my state is how rarely we can comprehend the world around us—I'm suddenly getting it: he is not persuading them of anything, he's just giving them pictures, images of great pain and great love. With the horrors, he is surrounding them, with the balm, he is curing them. It can be like this and it can be like that—he is showing them—which will you choose? Life is one, he is telling them, deaths are many and they're all yours. Which will you choose?

Suddenly, the man extends his arm around the woman's shoulders. He pulls her toward himself, hugs her tightly, and she puts her head on his shoulder.

Satie's lonely notes chime over us. Outside, snowflakes are levitating, undecided. Time has stopped and the world is holding its breath. Love is reappearing.

Azazel stands up and leaves. His wings are wound up around his shoulders so tightly that nobody can see them, not even I who knows that they are there. Some are born with wings, some without them—it has nothing to do with beliefs, or dreams, or delusions. Some can fly, some can't, that is all.

The man and the woman are sitting there, motionless. Another ricocheted light flows over their faces. I know them.

That woman is my mother. That man is my father.

They have never been here.

They have always been here.

They will remain in that room on the square.

They will be my religion.

I am driving again on Warwick Road. Perhaps I was right before—I shouldn't be returning here—but the brain keeps drilling until it finds a way to satiate its hunger. The rain has stopped, and now the wind is patrolling through the barren industrial zone.

I am driving slowly. The road is deserted, except for a few blackbirds that zoom through the streetlights like bullets from a machine gun drilling holes in the night.

At first I didn't see him, since the shadows have moved in the meantime and put a cloak on his shoulders. Now my lights are reflecting from the safety tapes on his coat and his body peels off from the wet painting that is the street.

I stop, pull the brake and leave the hazard lights blinking. I am sitting with my hand on the door handle for a few seconds and then I get out.

He is standing in the same spot where I left him. He looks relaxed as he watches me approaching.

"Hello," I say.

"Hello," he says.

"I don't know you."

"I don't know you."

"But we know each other."

"But we know each other."

I look at him, at his face, his eyes. He is serious. And he looks at me—I am serious. It dawns on me:

"If you are my reflection, how come we don't look the same?"

"I am not your twin," he says. "I'm a possibility of you."

I pause to think about it.

"I only have one? What happened with my

68

other options?"

"You should ask yourself, not me, about that," he shrugs. "Many wrong turns, many goings backward without thinking and without warning. Possibilities are fragile. We tend to die young. By the time you turn forty we are decimated. I am one of the two remaining," he says.

"I shouldn't be able to influence my future... You are talking in metaphors, right?"

He smiles. He's missing several teeth.

"Metaphors take precisely two ingredients. One to be covered and one to cover it with. The metaphor for life is death."

English is my second language.

"What is that other option?"

"Thanks. You look good, too," he says.

"What—irony as well? I thought you guys just had to scare us on sight."

"I am not an apparition," he says. "Don't judge people by the soil on their soles. You and I are parallel. I'm a possibility but so are you. I am fully physical. See this," he says and punches me in the nose. It isn't too strong but still hurts.

"Aw!"

I touch my nose. It's bleeding.

"Here," he says, pulling a paper tissue from another universe. It is recycled, but recycled from their junk.

"Thanks," I say. "Was it really needed?"

"There's nothing as sobering as a sudden collision with parallel reality," he says.

"So, may I know what is my other option?"

"I haven't seen her in a while," he shrugs. "I'm

not a prophet, I wouldn't know. But you can always die, if you wish."

He extends his hand and opens his fingers to reveal something small on his palm. It is rectangular and off-white and it takes me a few seconds to recognise an eraser.

"Just like that?"

"And why not? Life is being created, but it is also creating. Life is being destroyed, but it is also destroying. Look," he says and picks the eraser with his right hand. He waves it in the air a few times, up and down, the same trajectory. Underneath, there is now only a patch of condensed darkness. It makes me shudder.

"So I'll live?" I say.

"As long as you have options."

"That's great. I thought this was some sort of Purgatory, or something. You know — souls exploring the twilight zone while waiting for transportation."

"No, you will live," he says. "Go back now, and I'll take the car."

"He's coming to. Look, he's moving his lips, he's trying to say something!"

"Call the doctor! He is bleeding!"

"He's moving his head."

...

"Make a little room, please. When did it start?"

"We saw it only now, but judging by the amount it can't be long."

"Can you hear me? Nurse, wipe the blood from his nose, please!"

"Gde sam ja sada? Koji je ovo dan?" [1]

"Which language is that?"

"Foreign."

"Thank you, sir. You can get back to your ward now."

"Ja... Mislim da mi je sada sve jasno..." [2]

"Can you speak English, please? Do you understand what I'm saying?"

"Naš smisao... To sve... Mi smo samo krugovi na hladnom jezeru." [3]

¹ Where am I now? What day is it?
² I think it's all clear to me now...
³ Our purpose... All that... We are only circles on a cold lake.

DEATHROOM III

It's a brand new hypermarket and your eyes hurt. The shelves are shiny, the nickel on the baskets is glistening, the floor tiles are without bruises and reflect every lumen of the fluorescent ceiling light. The shop assistants still cradle hopes for a better future and don't show signs of being jaded and zombied. They've even persuaded you to take their loyalty card although you don't live here and you're faithful only to the roads.

Today's special are nappies for grown-ups. Two-for-one, and they have the size your mother would need. She's never used nappies, and normally doesn't need them, but her doctor has already spoken to you about that. At first you've refused to contemplate it—even the idea of a mother in nappies somehow seems wrong. Four legs in the morning, two at noon, three in the evening? Where do you put nappies when there are three legs?

Now you are tempted and you pick two packs of nappies and throw them into your shopping cart.

You can decide later, while strolling along the aisles, trying to avoid the red "Action!" signs. (It is a "Sale!" sign elsewhere, but this chain was bought by an Austrian daughter of a German company in the hands of a London investment fund owned by a Montenegrin narco-cartel. A journalist with the city newspaper has written about it and the locals immediately christened the building Koka. The journalist disappeared a week later, and has mostly not been found.) You always enter full of energy, with a firm plan of what to buy, but this place grabs you and sucks the will out of you, and after a while you just drag your feet behind the cart, a confused ox who has abdicated his right to pull. Soon you start feeling profound sadness. The hypermarket sadness.

Perhaps there is more than just that—you also cry at home, alone. When you return from the hospital you make yourself a coffee, you turn on your little red transistor radio, you open your computer trying to write something, you stare at the screen for some time, and then you start crying. These tears are not for others to see because they are not for others. You are crying for yourself, you are crying because you will be missed when you die. Because you won't be missed when you die. Those who love you will be suffering. Or, nobody will remember you. There will be no show. Draw your funny people in your notebooks, disproportional, perspectiveless, and don't think of reactions. There will be none. You will hand over your notebooks to someone a short time before you die, thinking—hoping—that they will pore over it, and because you've decided early on that only a person of a sensibility similar to yours would be able to decode what you meant in certain places, you've thought of a trick of how to obtain one such person: all your notebooks are written in a combination of Serbian and English, so most likely the researcher, or at least the cataloguer, will be someone of a Serbian origin. Your drawings inside are sometimes only doodles, though sometimes you are more ambitious. You've seen a few exhibitions where artists' sketchbooks were on display, and it's given special taste to everything exhibited, much more intimacy, as if you've been a close friend of the artist. At the same time it creates the illusion of you being the first person to open a pharaoh's tomb after a few millennia. The pleasure of discovery, the orgasm of opening, the eureka moment.

(You will bring some fruit to the hospital. Apples are strong candidates: perfect cubes, all identical, pleasantly red, attached to the branches of the cute plastic trees in aisle 132. Organic.)

And you imagine how it will be after your death: some small but distinctive gallery, a good curator who loves your work but also likes to be provocative, your drawings and your manuscripts and your digital media, and your photographs and snapshots, your videos and animations, your books, maybe a pair of your gloves, a hat, a pair of shoes if that curator knows you really well. Amidst all that— some serious, intelligent people walk slowly by your things, it's cold outside, the longer they stay the more they'll enjoy a tea or a coffee afterwards, perhaps a glass of red wine over some tapas or baguette & cheese; plenty of food for thought you've given them; in death you will be delivering more happiness than when you were alive—your small drawings give a special flavour. They make you more human, kinder, because you know that inevitably many of your notes will be perceived as misanthropic and then those uneducated, childish drawings will level you with the targets of your wrath. Your writings are your sins. Your drawings are your indulgences.

There will be no exhibition. Your work will be forgotten while you're still alive, and the long-ago-made decision to screw the retirement plans of all sorts, in all the countries where you've ever lived, will prove to be catastrophic. As you've seen in your nightmares, you'll be able to work until you die, your gods and blood vessels will remain permeable, but your oeuvre will not interest anyone. Books out of print, lines in your drawings only slightly better than 30 years before—who would care? Not to mention that around the time of your late years the whole world will be preoccupied with the latest agent provocateur, this singer who arranges roses around her pussy, such a rich symbol, virginity and thorns and blood and danger and the scent, the scent of eternal May, legs wide opened, awareness of your own sex, a rose by any other name, the Sleeping Beauty behind the wall of roses, menstrual blood rising from the earth, eruptions, ejaculations, the volcanoes of the body. Departments will get funding because of her, doctorates will be written, conferences in beautiful places will get organised, late night talk shows will dare, morning hosts will abstain. Your essay about her—based on the premise that the vase as an object is almost as old as the pussy as a subject, and that Nihil novum sub sole—will not be published. And that will be the end of you. There will be no exhibition.

(Oranges! A new invention: inside the peel there are two chambers. One contains pulp, the other juice laced with vitamins and caffeine. "We give you the whole fruit, and then some!" it says on the package.)

There will be no exhibition. And that is really why you cry.

Your tears are sincere, like when one listens to a ballad, or when one hides his face from the gravely ill. You are not performing sorrow, you are so tense that you are squeezing your bones and those tears come from them. You cannot explain that to yourself. You try, you give many explanations—and all of them stand, all of them are plausible—and yet you feel that something hasn't been mentioned. Perhaps something is unmentionable. Are you hiding something from yourself? Why are you crying? But seriously—

—why?

They are planning to add more sections to this hypermarket. You've read it somewhere but you can't remember where. There will be a gas station in the north-eastern corner, with a car mechanic next to it. Aisles 405 & 406 will give way to an access road.

But they apparently keep improving the experience. The small synthetic grass-covered area where they sell patio furniture has been made into a picnic zone. Shining, smiling assistants are lying on the grass passing mustard to each another, the brass lamps (2 for 1) producing "sunshine" around the area also cure muscle ailments, plastic sunflowers react to the sound of your voice, following you around with their fake heads covered with fake field dust, attracting very realistic plastic iBirds that can tweet, but can also play .mp3 files (designed in California, produced in China), and what looks like a group of birch trees surrounding the glade is a set of flexible 92" screens that can find and display any kind of virtual surrounding you crave, and is constantly connected to your social network of choice. The charming white puffy cloud up there is actually the computing cloud and it contains all the content you have ever produced:

> your diary, drivel,
> and X-rays, and snivel,
> your shames and your glories,
> love letters and stories,
> your poems and pictures,
> your passports and strictures,

> your warranty papers,
> the acerbic comments
> about rotten ex-colleagues,
> your sound recordings,
> videos, porn,
> your have-nots, belongings,
> your wheat and your corn.

The cloud belongs to the chain, so anything in it is not yours anymore, but—courtesy of the hypermarket—you can access your files at any time, minimum purchase required.

From here to the Pulmonary there are two sets of lights and neither are long—you arrive fast. You could have walked that distance, you could've parked the car either on the hypermarket parking lot or in the field in front of the hospital, but you drive. You drive everywhere around here. If you could, you'd enter this gigantic store in your car, drive between the blinding shelves, pull the handbrake on the corners, make your tyres screech when you see a cheeky derrière.

You are looking forward to the access road.

You drive everywhere around here. You park the car under a balding pine on the side of the driveway leading to the Pulmonary.

The draft kicks the hospital door from your hand and it slams against the stopper on the other side. You regret the noise but the elderly woman on a stretcher, who is pushed down the corridor by two frail and exhausted nurses, doesn't pay attention. She is clutching her own life, and is afraid that her hold is getting weaker by the minute.

You try to melt into the wall to let them pass by and then you hurry down the corridor.

Room 1 is right across from the nurses' room. It contains five beds and the patients admitted there are either in serious condition or need special attention for other reasons. All beds are taken, at all times. Your mother, in Bed 1, is in the corner to the left of the entrance. Along the opposite wall, under the row of tall windows looking at a small pine wood, are four more beds. The women in 2 and 4 are being readied for release, but the one in Bed 3 was brought here from another room two days ago and nobody is sure of her condition.

In Bed 5 there is a small woman with short grey hair. She's young but there is something ashen in her, something that reminds you of winter. She doesn't talk much to anyone—nurses included—and some of her relatives are always by her bed, except at night when everyone has to leave.

Your mother has a needle in her left arm. Colourless liquid is slowly dripping while she is staring at the ceiling. The two healthier women are reading. It's very quiet. The woman in 3 is sleeping, or pretending to sleep. She can hear only very loud sounds and is never in good mood—whether because she feels isolated, or because she's simply like that, you don't know. The large man and the tiny woman standing by Bed 5 are silent. I can't see the grey woman for them, and I'm trying not to look in her direction. Perhaps she is unwell; people tend to turn their heads and not look at dying people.

Dying is not a polite gesture. Everyone should retreat somewhere and do it discreetly. There should be an invention for dying at home. It should be a pedestal of some sort, a throne perhaps, and we should retreat into the deathroom, lock the door, sit on it and die there. Obviously, the machine has to have some sensor that would do the flushing once we're done. The tubing should lead to a parallel network for gathering bodies.

A small ceiling fan should suck up the 17 grams of nothing released in the moment of dying (they say this is the soul leaving its body, and this weight is the European average—some other locations show different values). From there it is fed into a network that ends somewhere in the Swiss Alps, in the giant underground vault where souls are catalogued for an American search engine, scanned and deposited for future perusal.

Another sensor would release the air freshener ("Dead souls leave an unpleasant smell. Our product is an odour eliminator and memory improver in one. Your beloved ones will remember you even more fondly than they normally would! Because you deserve it!" — Available in four distinctive versions: Baby Breeze, Bella Muerte, Pinions of Bliss and Angelica dei Occhi. For consumer info dial 0800 999, Mon to Fri 9 - 5. Conditions apply.) At the other end of the tubing system, a team of trained employees in white uniforms and with symbolic cardboard wings should separate bodies by religion, deeds and bank reports.

On the nightstand by your mum's bed is the non-invasive respiratory apparatus. It looks complicated, and expensive, and there are only two trained nurses who are allowed to switch it on or off. The diodes on it are blind now, and the rigid plastic mask lies on top.

You leave the fruit on the nightstand, next to the breathing machine, and you put the bag with the nappies inside the lower compartment. Almost everyone here has a tube protruding under their blankets and leading to a plastic bag full of yellow liquid, pushed deeper under their bed but still visible. Liquid dripping into people, liquid dripping out of them. Bodies—gurgling traps under the sink. A year ago, when your mother was in this same room, not a single patient had an external reservoir. But doctors prefer catheters this season.

You ask your mother if she wants to sit, but she refuses. You think you understand: it's the economy of view. It's not knowledge that can hurt you here, it's what you see that depresses you.

You sit on the edge of her bed, open an orange and put pre-cut slice straight into your mum's mouth. She smiles between the bites.

"I've had another argument with them," Mum says, munching the orange flesh. "My doctor had ordered them to put me under the mask, but to remove it in the evening, at eight o'clock, because she knows I can't stand it on my face overnight. And so they did: put it on and forgot about me, as usual."

You know this story. It hasn't happened today, not even during this current stay in the hospital. It has happened, though, it is not a fruit of her imagination, but the repetition is one of her symptoms. You switch off.

A nurse stops at the door, scans the room and leaves.

"In the evening, I couldn't stand the mask anymore. I felt like dying from all that misery. I'm waving my hands in the air, I'm crying under the mask. And this other patient from my room sees that I'm in distress and says, 'For God's sake, take it off Mila, you don't have to suffer like that!' And I say to her that I would take it off but I don't know how. 'Screw that,' she tells me, 'if you're in pain, just pull it off, make it easy on yourself.' "

You go to the door to throw the orange peel into the trash bin in the corridor. The nurse who had just been inside is talking to another, older one. The older one looks at Bed 5 and steps into the room. She tells the man and the woman to wait outside until she runs the regular check-ups. That's what you hear her telling them: the regular check-ups. You immediately know what she's doing: she's infusing a little sense of repetition to calm them down. Which means it's not good.

"And so I did: I pulled off the rubber tapes and somehow took the mask off," Mum says, "and I carefully put it on the nightstand, next to the machine. Eight o'clock in the evening has come and gone, nobody showed up to remove the thing as my doctor had instructed them, my conscience was clean. There was nothing for me to reproach myself with."

You sit again on your mother's bed, below her feet, and you try not to look, but it happens in the corner of your eye and what you don't see in detail you reconstruct from experience: the older nurse closes the door behind the two visitors—she is not telling you to go out because you are a fixture here, your mum's been here so many times that there are employees in this building that are novices compared to the two of you—and goes to Bed 5. She takes the grey woman's hand and checks on her pulse. She hurriedly exits, leaving the door open. The visitors don't come back in, they must have gone outside to take a break or talk to the others from their family (you've seen them when parking, there were maybe four or five people outside).

"It wasn't 15 minutes later, here comes the nurse on duty, a dark-haired woman, a small one, you must know her, a cocky witch. And she goes, 'Who did this, who took it off, how dare you, do you have any idea how much this apparatus costs...' "

The doctor on duty must have been already waiting, since she enters fast. She is taking off her stethoscope in stride and the moment she is standing by Bed 5 she is already listening to the woman's chest.

"And I tell her, 'Girl, you know what—my husband and I had bought that thing with the money that was taken off our salaries as obligatory contributions for building this hospital. All citizens who lived in this town at the time had to take part. We had built this hospital before you were born. So don't open your mouth too wide!' " Mother says, spitefully.

"Bring the defibrillator in here!" the doctor says. She turns around, sees you and asks you to leave the room.

"And she just kept quiet," Mum finishes her story.

You wipe her mouth with a paper tissue and turn to leave. Two nurses are entering the room, pushing some small machine on a movable stand. You have to wait for them to position it next to Bed 5 and you take a better look at the grey woman.

She is leaving quietly, probably heavily sedated. Her face is ashen, her eyes wide open, staring at the sheet crumpled next to her left thigh. She is leaning against the bunch of pillows piled up behind her. She already seems somehow smaller and lighter. Life vibrates, life is the antipode of stillness, and that constant vibration makes the living things look bigger than they are. The dead look shrunken because that dancing jelly is now frozen. They are focused in our eyes, the image of them is now sharp.

They don't move, they don't produce any sounds or actions, they will not cause any consequence, they will not invoke any emotions except the ones we've already developed for them— and those become conserved and preserved in us, frozen like their bodies, improved with time because optimism is just a product of poor memory. And—because we perceive life as the happy state—we will pity them and cry for them and weep with their family. And—because we are innately selfish—we will cry for ourselves, tears much heavier, because we now know how it will end.

The nurses are buttoning up their white uniforms. You presume it's part of the emergency code around here, but you chose to believe they are treating death with respect. When they are sending their patients off from here, they are angels, they are the last picture from this earth and perhaps the first image of the new life—they don't know, we don't know—and they want to be remembered as properly uniformed seraphs.

Death brings greyness into the room.

Black is the absence of all colours and white is the presence of all, in their full intensity. The grey of death is the one in which every colour is present but the intensity is lowered. That's the colour of restraint. It is white on the road to its end.

Death is the moderation and not annihilation.

When Death enters the room, all who are present get a momentary attack of madness. Although very short, it is a powerful and absolutely dark state of mind, and maybe from that eclipse comes the tendency to portray Death in black, and not from its relation to sorrow. What you feel is black although what you see is grey, like a fog in autumn in the valley by the river, and transparent so both sides can be seen through it, non-life from this side, life from the other side.

To die is a noun and not a verb. There is no process there, there is no doing. What looks like dying is only a very miserable life. Death is the moment of passing from one state of matter into another, and that moment is so infinitesimally short it cannot bear a verb.

We were flowing until now, we were rapids, we were roaring down the rocks. From now on we shall fall silently, the gentle white crystals of your memories, our state of life is Dead.

You see that border now in Room 1, and you see that your mother seems safe, and that you seem safe. You exit and close the door behind you. You walk down the corridor to the front door, you want to go outside and wait in the courtyard. Then you see the grey woman's family standing there, and you're afraid they would come to you and ask you how she was, and so you stand a little to the side from the door, invisible in the shadow, and watch them.

You know their immediate future. You know what will happen to them. You know the blow, you know the pain, and for a second you feel powerful.

The trees outside, and the thin grass, bring you back to reality. Not the people.

A few minutes later one of the nurses who was in the room appears from around the corner, still in full uniform. You ask with your eyes and she says,

"You can go back now. It's over."

She stops just before the door, her hand hesitating on the handle.

"I have to inform the family. The doctor has

asked me to," she says. She looks you pleadingly in the eyes, then sighs and exits.

"I hate this fucking world," she says quietly.

The door of the Room 1 is still closed. In the nurses' room opposite you see the doctor and the nurses who are putting together their report. You open cautiously. You don't know the etiquette for such occasions, nor the hospital rules, if there are any. You open very slowly, you don't know if there's maybe a piece of machinery left behind. You don't know if there's a soul somewhere in the room waiting to exit, waiting for someone to open the door now that all the handles are impossibly heavy.

On Bed 5 there is a bundle, a small parcel wrapped up in a white hospital sheet. It looks smaller than the woman who died there and for a second you wonder if it's her body at all. Maybe these are only sheets collected for cleaning, the pillowcases, the blankets.

You walk in, trying not to stare. The other patients are tense. The worst is not over. The relatives will come any moment now.

You come to your mother's bed—she's still staring at the ceiling—peel a banana without asking her and try to draw her attention away from the events by talking to her about something, but she interrupts and asks, "What just happened?"

"The woman in Bed 5 has just died," you say.

"We were friends," she says.

They were not.

They were.

Then a young woman enters, screaming with pain. She kneels by the bed and hugs the sheet. They have difficulty pulling her away from the body. Mum looks at you and says, "I can't allow myself to get shaken about everything."

You suddenly feel happy and with that your presence becomes inappropriate.

You promise to return later in the afternoon and you leave the room. When you exit the building and look downhill, towards the city, you see how greyness, thick around the hospital, slowly descends towards the first apartment buildings, a mile away. It looks thinner in the distance but it is spreading.

By this evening, life will clear the fog or the whole world will be dead.

You suddenly decide to go back to the hypermarket.

You want to buy some bleach and cocoa. You want to make a bomb that would scatter chocolate shrapnel when it explodes. Then the world would be one with its essence: looks like chocolate, tastes like shit.

And you also need bread and milk.

And you need that shine.

From the hospital to their parking there are two sets of lights and neither are long—you arrive fast. You could've walked that distance, you could've left the car under the balding pine, but you drive. You drive everywhere around here. If you could, you'd enter the hospital in your car, drive down the corridor, your tyres screeching, piss bags exploding, nurses screaming with excitement, patients—liberated—dancing.

You drive everywhere around here. You park the car under a giant billboard advertising memory improving pills.

There is a young woman standing alone just outside the entrance. She's supposed to be promoting some product or other, but everyone notices only her immensely sad brown eyes and her drooping eyebrows that turn her expression into elegy. When people come here, when they enter this hypermarket they feel blue and they don't even know why. That's how powerful her sorrow is, how contagious.

Perhaps that's the whole ploy: the only road out of sadness is leading by the till. Sad people carry their loot in bursting plastic bags. Now they approach the promo woman from behind, and her backside is much more optimistic than her face. It's a smiling bottom, it's a very positive, uplifting experience, a sprinkled donut. But when you pass by her, just keep going into daylight.

She will disappear if you turn and look at her.

POSTCARDS FROM PAST WINTERS

It was a day squeezed between bearable days. Clouds, heavy as a soaked nappy, pressed narrow houses hard against cobblestones, making the whole city look lower, ironing out smaller bridges, nibbling at the church towers, flattening cars and lampposts and the spirits of the few hurried pedestrians. Vermeer must have spent all the light there's ever been in Holland.

I was leaving the next day and Amsterdam was already slipping away, wrapping itself, shutting down, erasing colours and faces and smells, washing my footsteps away with relentless rain. There won't be a single memory left when I get home, I won't have anything to tell about this trip. Five days for nothing.

It was still too early to go back to my room and pack. I didn't bring much with me in the first place and I've only bought a few trinkets here: an old striped jacket at the flea market, an aluminium fountain pen, and a few singles—John Lennon,

Blondie, Kool and the Gang. Bette Davis Eyes. And a bag of tulip bulbs I had nowhere to plant.

I passed several empty cafés on Paleistraat and turned left into Nieuwendijk. The long street was full of small shops. I had a few guilders left and I was hoping to find some presents I could get away with back home.

The window of the tiny boutique next to a junk food joint was almost entirely hidden behind a SALE sign. The door hit a small brass bell hanging above it when I entered. Coat racks with dresses and blouses covered the side walls from ceiling to floor. On the tables in the middle, cardboard boxes were overflowing with accessories in orange and lime and grapefruit. I pushed my hood back and knelt down by a large box full of shawls, behind the door. A small brunette, probably my age, slowly walked closer to me and stopped a few feet away, respecting my right to pray to the gods of past winters. She watched me sift slowly through the heap, then got bored, went to the back of the store and changed the music. It was some slow R&B. Deep bass, wah-wah, all. A woman started singing. Her voice was deep and dark and smelled of musk.

Wah-wah. She's seen many lonely people who had decided to keep their pride and let love go. Her love went deeper than pride. Wah-wah.

I stopped rummaging through the box and moved closer to the speaker. The brunette suddenly said, "This weather makes me sleepy. Would you join me for a coffee?"

There was no hidden meaning in that. We were just two comrades under the bomber clouds.

We spent an hour sitting at the back of the store, talking about people and rain, about her home in West Germany, about catchers and the rye. There were only two customers during that time, but they didn't stay long. I was right: she was also 27.

When I stood up to leave—my hands full of tropical colours—she said:

"That song—I love it, too. Have you listened to Millie Jackson before?"

"I don't think that love goes deeper than pride," I said. "But sometimes I'm not sure. On rainy days especially."

She shrugged.

"Have you seen that movie 'Birdy'?" I asked.

"No."

"There is a scene there, when the two main characters talk. They're both war veterans. Birdy has gone nuts, and the other one's face got destroyed in Vietnam. He says to Birdy, 'And if you ask yourself, Birdy, how do I live now—I'm trying to live with a little dignity. And where there's dignity, Birdy, there's no sex.'"

She laughed.

"Who did you say was the singer?"

The brunette brought the cover and showed it to me.

" *Caught Up* by Millie Jackson? Never heard of it."

"It's not new, but there's a good record store a few doors towards the harbour," she said.

I pulled the hood over my head and stepped out into the rain.

They had the Millie Jackson album in the record store.

I went for a bite in a dark café with the view of a canal. The rain slowed down, and some children came out to play. One of them held a little red transistor radio to his ear. I watched them, trying to find a metaphor in that—the little children plus dead water in the canal—and then gave up. Exasperated, the metaphor came in and switched the stereo on. Gloria Gaynor started singing 'I Will Survive'. Oh, that.

I could've stuck my nails into the bark of the large tree outside, to become inseparable with the place. I could've chained myself to the bike rail. I hated going back to Prague. But we mostly get chained to the rain, and stick our nails into blackboards.

Sarah and I shared a rented pad a few hundred metres from the Old Town Square. It was in a small coach house, tucked in the back of a paved backyard, with ceilings too high for Kafka, too low for happiness. Sarah was a friend of a friend from Belgrade, and he gave me her address when I told him I wanted to go to Prague and do some research for my new book. She had a spare room, and didn't mind sharing the house with someone quiet. But my research stretched. As did Sarah's studies at the Film Academy. I found a temporary job as a correspondent of a magazine in Belgrade—not much money, but Prague was kind if you knew where to search for kindness.

We were like sisters. Or brothers, depending on whose rainy day it was. We kept each other.

One deaf afternoon I went into Sarah's room, hoping that she would help me crumple a few hours, and an unknown woman was there. Sarah introduced Anya, a colleague from the Academy. I couldn't take my eyes off her, and she kept sitting on the edge of her chair, looking occasionally at my lips. Sarah easily saw through us, and half an hour later said she had to study and kicked us out. We went to my room and—without saying a word—started devouring each other as if the whole life before that was just a long hunger.

After some time, she got dressed and left. There were no promises, no questions, not much talk. At the door, she wrote my number on a piece of paper and threw it into her bag. I saw many such pieces inside. I hoped some were not lovers.

The next day I went to Sarah's room again. I wanted to hear more about Anya, but she knew nothing. They met at the Academy. Anya was the babe in the group. Many men made passes at her, but Anya was strange about her choices. Sometimes she chased the good men away; sometimes she went with idiots without much talking.

That had been three months ago. The silence with Anya continued. We talked only while making love. Every time she called to say that she would drop by—which was once or twice a week—I closed the windows in advance. And I had to dim the lights. Anya didn't even want to take her coat off if there was too much light. The deep shadows of her breasts, the dark clouds of her skin, the drops of light on her body in motion—it was a stuff of myths, a minor religion. With such body I'd walk naked, anywhere, anytime, and not ask for cover. I did not quite understand her being shy. Maybe that's what she wanted—to not be understood. Or maybe she toyed with me. That thought disturbed me—I had ended up as a lottery ticket inside her bag.

Had I placed a tub filled with ink at my doorstep, and covered the floor of my room with paper, at least I would have known the steps, I would have had a map. I had nothing.

Maybe I wanted nothing. I did not sever my other relationship when this thing with Anya started. I kept seeing Milena once or twice a week as well. Milena wasn't mine—she was married, but her husband has been working in Russia for the past few years. I was only her replacement body. Anya wasn't mine. I was her body, too. Body, body, nobody. We're all like Russian dolls: a lover inside a lover inside a lover, seven times like that. Painted in romantic hues, golden dots on our scarves, rounded asses, rosy tan.

Instead of feeling lucky for having two good women to save me from loneliness—which in this world is a given and everything else a miracle—I felt like a roadside chapel. But, nervous or not, I could see that Anya was gaining ground fast, much faster than would let me feel safe. I knew that by the way I started noticing the time between her visits.

And then, a day or two before I travelled to Amsterdam, Sarah came to my room for the usual morning coffee. It was raining outside.

"When did you see Anya last?" she asked, trying to make a sugar cube from the small tray jump into her spoon.

"A week ago. Longer. Why?"

"How are you two?"

I looked through the window at the old stones in the yard.

"Like rain and gutter," I said. "You know who's who."

"I hear that Anya is becoming a legend," Sarah said, still trying to hypnotise that cube.

Some local football star had thrown a party. At some point, when everyone had gotten drunk, the host had said how women loved giving head more than men receiving it. Because, according to him, women mostly didn't know how to do it, and guys reckoned it was better to remain silent. Then Anya, also very drunk, had proposed a bet—she would do it to him, right there, and if it took him more than five minutes to come, she would pay him a hundred. Otherwise, he owed her a thousand.

"Anya earned that thousand," Sarah said. The cube plopped into her cup.

I bet she had.

I decided to avoid Anya's calls. Not that there were many. Actually, I don't know if she's called at all—I stopped answering the phone and then I came here, to Amsterdam. The numbers were drawn and my ticket didn't win.

Outside, the metaphors and the rain stopped. I paid the bill and left.

Later that evening, when I opened the bag to start packing, I discovered that my new fountain pen had bled ink into the breast pocket of my new jacket.

My return to Prague was uneventful. There was a letter from my editor and another from my mum. I sent a travel article to Belgrade. I gave my present to Sarah, but she had to hurry with some assignment and we didn't talk properly.

Then, three or four days after I returned, the doorbell of our apartment woke me up one night. It took me two minutes to understand that someone was at the door, and another two to remember where the door was in the house I was sleeping in now. I looked at my watch—it was 2:30 in the morning and Prague was quiet outside. Someone kept ringing. I found my jeans and stumbled to the door. Anya stood in front. She was drunk.

"I came to you," she said.

"I can see that. You shouldn't have."

"You don't *geddit*. I *came* to you."

"Yes, I do get it. You shouldn't have."

I took her by the hand and led her back to the gate. The taxi was still waiting on the steep narrow street, and the driver stood next to it with his door open. He had seen how drunk she was and wanted to make sure she stayed somewhere safe.

"I don't know her address," I said to the driver. "If she can't remember where she lives, drive her to where you picked her up."

"I don't think she has any money," he said.

"Here, I'll pay."

"I don't need your money," the driver said. He helped Anya get into the back seat, closed the door gently, and drove off.

Sarah stood at the door to her room, next to the entrance.

"Anya?" she asked.

"Fuck her."

"We're throwing away such babes? We'll be sorry when we get older. Like, tomorrow," she said.

"Fuck you, too," I said, and slammed the door to my room. Then I opened it again. "Come inside for a drink. I won't be able to sleep, anyway."

Sarah sat across from me, on the old rocker by the door. She was in her nightgown and had the orange shawl wrapped around her shoulders. I got away with that one. It didn't look bad on her, actually. I poured two glasses of red and put the needle onto whatever was on the turntable. Deep bass, wah-wah.

If loving him was wrong, then she didn't want to be right. Wah-wah. If she couldn't see him when she wanted, she'd see him when she could. Wah-wah.

"Is this the record you've bought in Amsterdam?" Sarah said.

"Yeah, the same day I bought your shawl, just across the street."

"You never told me how that last trip was. Was there a girl for the sailor?"

"No, there never was. It's just... I don't know, I just have to go there from time to time."

"It's that nice, ha?" said Sarah, watching me across the edge of her glass.

"The first time I went there I was 21. I was still living back in Belgrade. Something just clicked. People usually go there for sex and drugs. I tried both, but the weed was a downer, the girl was a bummer."

"So you go for the architecture?"

"Irony is illegal after midnight. No, I'm going there because that's the place where I'll live after I die. I think differently in Amsterdam. An ordinary walk—in other cities I just hit a street and I admire. I subscribe. There, I walk a little, and then there's a canal and a bridge over it, my thoughts are interrupted, they become like Morse code. And that dead water below my feet..."

She remained silent.

"Large windows without curtains. Applied philosophy."

"And, of course, you stare," she said.

"I stare in order to learn something."

"So why do you live here, in Prague?" Her voice was almost flat. There wasn't a sting in it, just a trace of reproach.

"Ah, that's the story of my life. When I lived in my hometown it wasn't far from Belgrade, where I wanted to live. I sneak in, then I conquer."

She chuckled. "If Belgrade was the place where you wanted to live, why didn't you stay there?"

"I came too late. By the time I moved, my head was someplace else."

"But you've been to Amsterdam, like, ten times in the last two years."

"Yes, but if I move there I might break the spell. My head travels by separate trains."

"You're fucked up."

"I know."

"What's with Anya?"

Really—what's with Anya?

I tried to say something I could get away with. An orange sentence, perhaps, a lemony joke. It didn't come.

Wah-wah. Was she wrong to hold on to the

best thing she's ever had? Wah-wah.

Sarah downed the rest of her wine and put the glass down. It was past three already, and she went to her room. I switched my hi-fi off.

The morning came reluctantly, weak, pale, insecure, unable to carry its shine. It wanted to call in sick but needed money.

I couldn't stand myself in that greenish light. Anya never asked for promises, never gave any. I should be grateful to her for sharing with me.

Sarah gave me Anya's number. Nobody answered. I went for a long walk across the river, but the wave of tourists cut me off from my own thoughts and I returned home sooner than I had planned. I read a Carver book. I called a few more times. She answered around ten in the evening.

"Look, I'm sorry about the last night. I wasn't alone."

I didn't know why I lied. Maybe because I thought that in our transitory tango such an excuse would be acceptable.

"You got me confused. I should've said I had someone in my room, but somehow I couldn't," I said.

"No, I am sorry," she said. "It wasn't okay to drop in just like that. And I was rather drunk. I don't have a clue what I was thinking."

"Would you like to come over now?"

She paused a little.

"I'll take a taxi."

Twenty minutes later she was at my door. I switched the lamp off. We went to bed. We talked.

We lay silent. Talked. Lay silent. A beam of milky light lay on her thighs, but I wasn't sure if the milk came from the outside or from her skin. The silhouettes of her breasts looked like the sides of a bridge leading to the main street of Anya, the one between her brain and her crotch. I needed light on that street. I needed to see if I was there.

My hand found the switch and I turned the bedside lamp on. She tried to cover herself, but I saw them: her hips and thighs were covered with long, wide scars. I bent over, removed her hand, and kissed one of the rough lines on her left side.

"You don't need to be ashamed of them. They're not ugly, and you're the best babe I've ever known, with or without them."

She leaned on her elbow, and there was a sudden look of dead calm on her face.

"What do you know about it?" she said. "I was sixteen when I survived that crash. My spine was hurt badly; I had to spend five months wrapped in plaster, not sure whether I'd walk again. What do you know about it? When they bring you bedpans for five fucking months, night and day? When the man I loved died in the car with me, while we waited for an ambulance? What do you know about it all? How can you know about how it feels when an old pervert, this nurse, comes at night to jerk off all over you, and you can't even move, and you don't want to scream because that's the only proof you're alive? What the fuck do you know about it? You like my scars? These are not scars, these are the postcards from the worst place I've ever been to."

She got up and started dressing. The most

beautiful body I have ever seen. She put on her black stockings and then pulled them up to attach them to the suspenders. The last time ever in my room.

"Anya, perhaps I loved you."

"Perhaps I loved you, too. Tonight—probably. But we both got scared shitless from it. And now it's too late anyway."

The next evening I hopped on the train to Amsterdam. I left both large bags on the floor by the seat. They were heavy and the train was almost empty. I stood at the window in front of my second-class compartment, staring at the dirty platform, waiting for the train to leave.

Sarah will do fine without me. She can find someone else for that extra room. The magazine in Belgrade will probably want me still when I move to Amsterdam. My dad's infarct went relatively well, Mum said. He will be out of the hospital soon. The doctors said it had nothing to do with his Parkinson's. The medicine is progressing every day.

Two hookers passed by, going to get some food at the kiosk. A cop nodded to them. Two Albanians were lifting an old oven into the coach of an international train parked on the next track. A woman leaning on the window, talking to them, fixing the scarf covering her hair. A sudden blow of wind carried her scarf toward me, and then the wind stopped, and it floated before my eyes for a moment—an ugly, lime-coloured thing someone got away with—before one of the men caught it. Then I turned my head towards the locomotive, because I felt a gentle pull, and the wheels started clicking over the urine-soaked ties. Under the yellow light along the railroad, the tracks shone like scars.

14 Years

You don't know what you're doing.

You don't know who you are.

You enter the room, and in the middle there's a long table covered with green cloth, with cheap office chairs around it. Seven doctors are sitting at the table, more women than men but the number of either gender is not 1 and it's not divisible by 2, reports and folders are strewn around, there are pieces of paper on the floor. You instantly recognise there's been a pillow fight but—this being a hospital—pillows are filled with shredded reports about the patients who had died. Some names are still visible on tiny strips. The permeating smell of disinfectants makes you nauseous. The doctors' faces are cold and you seek a friendly look or a gesture that is non-threatening. In vain. None of them invite you to sit down, although there are plenty of free chairs lined up against the walls.

"We have called you because we have some good news," says a male doctor whose bald top is poorly concealed with whips of yellowing hair.

You fear him.

"After 14 years in our hospital, your mother is cured," he says.

The fear goes away and now you hate him.

You think of how ridiculous this scene is, how simplistic. There's no need even for waking up. You don't have to turn around in your bed—this is such an obvious dream, such a lousy script.

Disgusted, you exit, and the outside of the hospital is the inside of your skull. The buildings in the street are painted in decaying green. Someone who wanted to glue new posters up tried to peel off the layers of old ones, and gave up. One long, curving patch was torn off, leafing in the wind, revealing the layers underneath, many layers, old Sundays, dead singers, dance fads that are now left for beer bellies and bald heads, choirs from which the little boys had been recruited, silent, obedient little boys, their annuli their calendars, like promises given to their parents and them, the immaculate printouts of distant worlds, the fading wall paint, stucco, bricks, dicks, glue, cunts, snuff, stuff—we have that all. All on our wall whose virginity never was; and the woman sitting in the front row in a café has a naked shoulder and a slender, white, impeccable neck and the thought kisses travel from your mouth to the curve of her shoulder; and a woman will pass by—a hoarse voice, a horse's ass, the legs in nets, nett IQ 138, a smart woman, sexy but unsexed by the blandness of this forgotten street; and the parking officer straightens his cap because he has more authority when Hitlerian, Goebbelsian, a cyanide capsule on his lapel, his son has opened a small business in a small town in Italy—the Chinese on the left, the whites on the right, their silk just like the Italian, like Polo, St Marco, Piazza, doge, longitude taken, latitude given, clocks still unreliable, don't travel yet, don't discover anything, trust me— everyone's better undiscovered, nude, unchristened, whimpering on the edge of the world he's afraid of, trembling, shaking, drawing waves in the air...

Your anger and your bitterness wake you up.

There are seven naked people sitting in front of you. They must be some kind of governing body of this naturist camp, tired after a long session, since they display the kind of behaviour that you remember from the long meetings in advertising companies where you used to work: a man is holding his hand high at his thigh, absent-mindedly touching his limp penis with his thumb, occasionally gently scratching his testicles; a woman pushes her large right breast up with the back of her hand; a man brings two fingers of his right hand to his neck, making a hook with them, and then runs that hook across his neck as if cutting his throat.

The papers have disappeared. Not entirely— they have a few sheets each in front of them and pens at the ready—but the featherlike chunks on the floor and elsewhere are gone. The table is a large piece of flat rock. There is a little red transistor radio on the side, and Satie is flowing from it, discreetly.

"We should celebrate such an interesting achievement, such—if I may say—a feat of medicine," the balding man says.

He has an unusually small member. You've seen religious paintings with bigger organs.

"And we would, in normal circumstances. However, the circumstances are far from normal."

Another man puts his hand on his thigh and scratches his testicles. You suddenly understand their moves: they are not aware that they are not clothed.

"Your mother's respiratory functions are adhering, it seems, to their own laws of physics. With our other patients—administering oxygen increases their saturation levels and lowers carbon dioxide in their blood. With her, carbon dioxide shoots through the roof. Everything is the opposite of expected. Do you understand what this means?"

He looks at you with mild interest. It is a rhetorical question. He is sure that you would not be able to comprehend what his words meant, but he is resolved to watch a lower form of life make an intellectual attempt.

He should really do something about his size.

"You had to stand on your heads while trying to cure her?" you offer.

At that moment the side door open and a procession of patients and their families enter. In pious silence they march to the desk, put their presents for the doctors on the flat rock, turn and leave. Not a word is uttered, not a question asked. Two or three women sigh as they put pieces of jewellery on the table, and some of the men leaving brown and blue envelopes don't seem too happy, but everything goes in perfect order. The doctors—if they are doctors at all, because by now you are fully aware of the absurdity of this whole dream and how nothing is to be taken for its face value here—pretend that they don't see anything, nothing at all.

They stare through the people, or check their fingernails with focused interest.

The last patients leave their offerings and close the door behind them. Nobody is looking at you but you feel their gaze. You think that their inner eyes are scanning you and you decide to show them your inner dick. But on the surface you take a leather bracelet off your left wrist, the only piece of adornment you have on your body, and leave it on the rock, among other objects.

"Ha!" the bald doctor claps his hands. At first you think he is happy because of what you just did, but no—he is reacting to your words, he is continuing your conversation before the procession had entered. "Ha!" he says again, because your break interrupted him the first time, "a good idea! Standing on our heads? Maybe that would be even better? Maybe the concentration of fluids in our skulls would increase the energy levels to no end. Let me try."

He stands up, steps on his chair, then on the table and, in spite of his large belly, turns his body upside down with ease, sways for stabilisation for a while, and then stands on his head, his body straight and balanced. His phallus is now absurdly long and reaches to his forehead and he has to blow it aside every few seconds, as it gets entangled with the remaining strands of his hair. Surprised, you realise that erection has something to do with the gravity and that, when there is one, a person is not on Earth but on the Moon.

"No, I'm afraid it's not working," he says after a while, and sits back in his chair. He shrinks back to normal.

"What we had to do," he continues talking to you, "was to suck the air out of your mother's lungs. That was the brilliant idea that cured her. We've noticed that anomaly with the carbon dioxide first, and then started paying attention to other elements of her blood tests, plus urine and all, and we saw that the pattern was being repeated. Then, by pure chance, we've discovered that there was a field of sub-pressure in the room where your mother was lying. We couldn't believe our instruments at first, but we did repeat the measurements and the results were stable: she indeed created an area of lower atmospheric pressure around her. How? She sucked the air from her surroundings. She couldn't create a vacuum, of course, but it was enough to create a stable field of low pressure."

You are in awe now. It doesn't matter if this is a dream or a poorly written script—they are onto something interesting, possibly something big. If a mother is a black hole, then her child is a star.

"How come nobody noticed that before?" you ask. "Why haven't I noticed that?"

"Ah, that's the ingenuity of it all!" he says. "You see, had she been able to do it in a more powerful way, you'd have noticed. You'd have felt as if suffocating. But on the level that she did suck the air, it actually created enjoyable effects for everyone around her. You must have felt pleasantly sleepy, right?"

You nod. He smiles broadly.

"Fields of low atmospheric pressure bring clouds and sometimes storms, but they also bring moderate temperatures. And what is more calming than hiding at home with your dear mum while storms are raging outside, ha?"

He looks genuinely happy just thinking of this. And you start remembering. People would suddenly start arguing around your mother. Not with her—around her. At first, when you noticed this, you thought that she was somehow manipulating people, making them confront one another for reasons beyond their comprehension, but then you had to admit that it happened even when she didn't say a word. So, thunders—yes.

Sleepy? You've felt sleepy many times while with her. But you thought it was because being in the company of your mother soothed your nerves on a very primitive, subconscious level. Her voice, her rhythm of speech, her choice of vocabulary—it was all very old-fashioned, and you thought that it caused drowsiness the way that watching a period drama caused you to slow down and become comfortable.

While you're thinking about this, the doctors start removing the offerings from the table. They don't make any moves except with their eyes, yet the things pile up before each one among them. It seems to be a fair distribution, until a scalpel flies across the table and makes a cut in the shoulder of one of the male doctors. At the same time a watch box disappears from before him and reappears on one of the other piles. The man who was cut doesn't blink, but hardly a few seconds later a plastic tube of a large catheter snakes underneath the rock and finds its way under the skirt of one of the women. She hardly winces when the tube finds the opening on her body but she frowns when a golden necklace goes up in smoke. Still, she remains silent.

By the time this is over, you've changed your views on the world in general and your situation in particular. You now realise that the room you're in is a desolate place with walls painted green. Under the wide window the patches of paint are peeling off. Empty plastic cups almost cover the table. There is a basin in one corner, a small black and white television on a fridge in another, and there is a sick plant by a sickening bed. It is all much more realistic now, perhaps completely realistic—you don't know, you haven't seen that particular room before. Then you notice a note on the wall: "Used dreams have to be deposited in safety containers!" Oh, right: you've heard about such rooms, but you've thought they were off limits for visitors.

"All in all," the doctor says, "your mother is well now and at first we intended to release her from the hospital in a day or two."

He has morphed into a giant truncheon. You find it hard not to laugh in his face. Of course, there is still a face, and a body, but he is a truncheon. The rest of the men and women are fine, except for the two who fought, who are now lying face down on the table.

"However, having in mind that she has been here for the past 14 years, you surely must organise things at home and find someone to help her. She will be very weak when she gets out and will need physiotherapy. So we will keep her here for another month. That is all the time we can give you, I'm afraid."

The rest of the doctors burst into laughter. "He's afraid!" they say, slapping their thighs and doubling with guffaw. They stop as abruptly as they started, stand up next to each other and start singing:

"Heart attacks and lightning—very, very frightening!"

"Mama mia!" you say. "Mama mia, let me go!"

"We will not let you go!" they sing.

"So it's true: you are all—"

"Insane?" asks Truncheon.

"No. Frustrated artists. How did you end up fixing people?"

Truncheon stares at his black boots.

"To be precise, we didn't *end up*," he says, at last. "We *started* by fixing people. Then we discovered we had so much to say about the state of being human, so much that is universal, and that is what makes art, no?"

"Hm," you say. "Yes and no. You know about blood and guts and nerves and flesh. Yours is the art of decay. But there is something that we cannot comprehend, something that holds it all together and at the same time is created and fed by its parts—"

"Skin."

"No, deeper than that. What about ideas, visions, dreams, hopes? You can't stick a needle in my fears. You can't operate my depression. I wish you could Botox my imagination, but you can't."

"We are working on it," Truncheon says, frowning.

"Yeah? How?"

"We are experimenting with suppositories that boost vanity," he admits.

"They're called the opportunists," you explain.

Truncheon looks ashamed. His shoulders stoop, he shrinks a bit.

"You don't get art by plugging a catheter into a brain," you tell him. "It is more than guts."

"But guts are part of it," he says.

"Yes," you agree without much enthusiasm.

"Perhaps your brilliant, sad poem comes from your body anticipating pain, because you don't know that there are malign cells travelling down your veins, but the body does," he says, full of energy.

"Sad poems are shit," you nod.

"And with decaying kidneys you won't write much," he says, erect again and grinning.

You shake your head, dark as a cloud.

"Have you noticed how close are art and chart?" he asks.

You frown at this. Cheap.

"Listen," he says, readying to go, "I find you to be a sympathetic character. I presume all this with your mother is taking its toll on your nerves. If you wish, go somewhere, take a vacation. We can keep her here for another 14 years if you wish. What do you say?"

"I have to think about it. I'm thin with money."

"Sell a story. Or a kidney. Depends on where you want to go, but the kidney will hurt less. Just don't forget that you also need to buy a scuba set—for you or for anyone who'll be taking care of your mother. There won't be any air in her vicinity."

You nod.

"I have a surgery to perform now. Nurse, please."

A young woman with black hair takes a large surgical mask out of a cupboard, tears the package apart and rolls it down his head and shoulders. He waves at you, opens the soft curtains of the operating theatre and stops for a second before the darkness ahead. Than he rushes in, headlong, into the unknown.

You go out, and finally, finally you know where you are, where in life, in thoughts, in time, in Universe. The longitude is taken, the latitude given, clocks are still unreliable, don't travel yet, don't discover anything, trust me—everyone's better undiscovered, nude, unchristened, whimpering on the edge of the world he's afraid of, trembling, shaking, drawing waves in the air and the waves of his body are resonating in space, creating invisible temples that fill with pain and flame—

—because—

—that's all we are: pain & flame.

Cups full of brain, spittoons
full of shame and
green and yellow snot,
paper flying back, higher, still higher,
rising, uprising, armed, legged, fire, naked thoughts and shoulders. And
always
there is someone fighting for breath whose pain & death will not touch a cell in your world but will shake mine to the core, someone whose arms make the brackets of my equation.
Always.

The corpses are on the street, the beauty of the revolution, the revolution revving up, it's televised, radiographed, and it's shipped back to the captain who refused to step again onto his sinking ship. News entering my mind like earth worms returning me to the pixels I was made of.

The morbid green is now gone. For you forever. But you are now me.

Everything is remarkably quiet. It feels like a Sunday morning's walk through the narrow streets of Mayfair. Those perfect façades, those loot bags, grandpa was a governor of an island, killed a few Tarzans, black Janes galore, skies were softer then, God was closer there, and you take a picture, and the light cyan dressing over everything makes it all sail straight into nostalgia, and nostalgia is gilded and great, it is admitted, it is fine, dust, silk, Oriental carpet over Occidental accidents waiting to be hidden. Three knots on my back when I see it all, find them and I'll come into your world, come in your memories, in your brain.

I was here with Anne, she took me out for a dinner, and it was a fine French place—I was smoking at the time and she sat me outside, under an awning, and she was freezing because of me; later I visited the Pulmonary—my mother there for the first time—and when I went out for a smoke a woman who was hooked onto an oxygen tank came out to beg for a cigarette from me. Dear Anne! But I haven't published anything since then, and so nobody's taking me out for lunch anymore. Spin a story, get some food.

Those façades of Mayfair, those quiet streets where reality is invisible and cameras yell at you, a sniper installed next to each one. Those tarts, those women of service, the porcelain maids with breasts the size of a bloomer, organic, all the silicone locally sourced. Like the head of a bold woman entering the Academy the other day—her perfect head, pleasant, respectful, proportional, and her bell bottom, and you couldn't help but imagine seating her in front of you, on a perfect Persian silk carpet, a lazy latte, the shushed sounds through the triple-glazing, and offering yourself to her silent mouth, a mouth that serves no other purpose, because she keeps silent about everything, she has, she will—there's always been someone close to her who craved for discretion, so she obliged.

A man is coming around the corner. He is thin and has dark face, white hands, Nagasaki eyes and Babylonian sandals. He walks straight at you, determined, a man with an idea and purpose, with authority, yes he can, he has your future and he will lead you there.

"I don't know what I'm supposed to feel," you tell him. "I don't know what I'm doing."

"Calm down," he says.

"I am calm," you say, "it's just that I need some directions. This is your show, after all."

"My show, your stage," he says amicably, but he's boiling on the inside, you can see it. "Anyway, this is the final scene, so don't panic."

"Final what?"

"You've heard me," he says, rearranging the trees in the small park adjacent to us with his black hands. He tilts his head, critically judging his work, then pushes back the façade of a coffee store until the street widens in that area. He looks happier now and claps his hands. Surprisingly, it sounds like thunder.

"How did you do that?" you ask him, in awe.

"I've sampled the thunder that killed a

shepherd," he smiles.

Down at the bottom of the street, the iron gates of the tube station open and a river of people starts flowing towards you. This is sudden, and feels threatening. You and the man are the only figures in the path of the crowd—just the two of you against everyone.

You are trying to find his hand.

"Stay," he says. "Calm down. Stay, don't move. You just watch them, your face doesn't twitch, doesn't show emotion. This is very important: no emotions *at all*."

He is watching you from the side, making sure you're following his instructions.

"Stand by me, clench your fists, look them straight in the eye. Fire when you see the white."

"Fire with what?" you ask him.

"Fire with your memories, of course," he says.

And indeed, since they haven't been part of your past, they can't become part of your present, and just by watching them you make them disappear. Only a few of them remain—those who had sunglasses on—but they turn into quiet people going after their own business and do not threaten you anymore.

"Fantastic!" the man says. "You've done well."

"Good directing, maestro," you respond kindly. "You were quite invisible."

"Thanks," he says, smiling again. "Let's go."

"Where to?"

"Where to? This is it. This is the end. You have to sign off now."

You stare at him, expecting him to laugh and

paint the joke funny, but he's serious.

"What end? Who are you?"

"I've had as many names as there have been people on Earth," he says.

"God?"

He doubles with laughter. He's getting on your nerves. Enough is enough.

"No," he says, "not God. My power was always real and brutal. *I'm your father*," he says in deep voice, and almost chokes laughing. "Seriously. Let's go. Follow me."

The applause starts slowly. At first a clap here, a clap there, slow and hesitant, and then more palms catch up and carry, ever more, until it thunders all around you, echoing down the peaceful street, which is deserted again.

"They loved it," the man says, smugly. "You've given them a good show. Congratulations."

"Are you serious? You are. But how can this be my end? This is just a dream."

"No, it's not. That's your life. You took it for a dream, because it hurt. By the way," he tells you over his shoulder, "pay attention: all tenses of hurt are the same. Hurt. Think about it.

Hurt.

Hurt.

Hurt."

HOTWIRE

Taking the short story for a ride on the wild side...

HOTWIRE is a series of short-story collections published by Nine Arches Press in paperback form. A chance to discover some of the best new short-story talent out there and to lose yourself in short fiction that excites, challenges and provokes its readers.

Since 2008, Nine Arches Press have published thirty poetry and short story books and pamphlets, including titles which have won the East Midlands Book Award and were chosen as the Poetry Book Society Pamphlet Choice in 2011. As publishers, they are dedicated to the promotion of work by both new and established writers, and the development of a loyal readership for contemporary short fiction and poetry. Find out more about Hotwire and Nine Arches Press by visiting their website at www.ninearchespress.com or by scanning this QR Code:

studio harringman

Studio Harringman is a multi-disiplinary creative studio based in East Sussex. For our clients we serve as a complete creative resource; strategy, design and production. We have over 30 years experience in design, branding and advertising. Our client list includes BBC, Thames Television, Universal Pictures, Home Office, Revlon, Warner Brothers, Fremantle and the Shaftesbury Theatre. Run as a family business, the studio was founded by Gary Harringman in 1999 with James Harringman joining the company in 2009. We believe in a world where anyone can publish, quality will always shine through. **www.studioharringman.com**